THE WITCH'S REUNION

A Witch Between Worlds #3

EMMA GLASS

A WITCH BETWEEN WORLDS…

In the wake of Clara Blackwell's departure, magical disasters strike the vampiric Earth.

Atop a tower during an unnatural winter, Elliott Craven grieves. Unable to turn back time to reverse his mistakes, the vampire lord descends down a dark and harrowing path. The broken vampire rules his kingdom with a cold, iron fist that only tightens with the passing year—all too aware that distracted enemies loom in the darkness, ready to wreak their vengeance.

Meanwhile, the heartbroken Clara struggles to adjust to her old life. As the months fly by and her dreams grow in danger, she falls ever deeper into fraught despair. Little does she know what secrets hide in the impossible amulet around her neck—and how far she must suffer to see her Elliott again.

The separated lovers are destined for a collision course that will change everything—and with disaster everwhere, their reunion will set an *unbelievable chaos* into motion...

PROLOGUE
CLARA

I was cold and shivering in a quiet room.

The door opened behind me. I barely noticed as the therapist they sent me stepped back into view, pressing a warm, fresh cup of tea into my hands. She took her seat at the table and looked at me with that curious, relaxing stare that people in her position tend to give—especially the ones employed by police departments. It didn't have the intended soothing effect on me.

It was penetrating, like she was picking me apart.

I didn't like it. I didn't like *her*.

"You're scared," she nodded. "It's okay."

I pulled the draped jacket closer around myself.

"It's perfectly fine to be scared, Clara," she repeated. "You've been through a lot these last few weeks. I can tell that, just looking at you."

You have no idea, I thought to myself.

"You don't have to talk if you don't want to, not right now. But I *do* have to take some notes down. We need to get to the bottom of this." The therapist glanced down at the notepad in front of her seat on the table. "Clara, you've been missing, what, three weeks? Four?"

The warm tea tasted bitter and cheap. But it offered a little heat, so I wrapped my fingers tighter around the cup and soaked up the feeling.

"The officers outside are nice. They want to let you go, but they need me to ask you some important questions first. They just want to make sure if there is anyone to be punished for what happened to you..." She looked back up from her notes. "...And if justice must be served."

I sipped my tea silently.

"That's all we want. Justice." She repeated with a slow nod. "Isn't that what you want too, Clara?"

I didn't answer; she moved on.

"Let me state the facts, as we have them right now. At some points, I'll throw in what I think. I want you to try and tell me if I've gotten anything wrong—I'll change my words and keep going. I can talk; you can listen."

The therapist smiled. "Does that sound okay?"

"I'd like to leave," I replied sadly.

Her smile faltered. "The police are quite insistent on a statement. They have a few theories on what happened, and they're ready to make an arrest."

Make an arrest? **What** *arrest?*

"So, here's how we have it..." The therapist glanced at her notes again for a moment. "Clara Blackwell, you went missing the day of Thursday, June the 21st. Your stepfather states that you left the house for school at around 7:30AM. You took the bus—there was a driver who recognized you from the news, he came forward to confirm that much—and he bumped you off of that the bus for what he called, '*rowdy behaviour.*' From that point you just, well... vanish." Her penetrating eyes flicked to me. "Disappeared straight off the face of the Earth."

I nodded quietly, betraying nothing.

You don't know how right you have that last part.

"You turn back up around 11:45AM, roughly three and a half weeks later, on July 16th—just two hours ago—on the edge of a lake." With a frown, she gazed at her notes again. "According to this, in the old Broadmoor Park, here in town. Our friend, the bus driver, could not recall exactly *where* he thought he asked you off the bus, but that's still within the possibilities he offered the police."

I knew it was coming when she shifted her gaze. She wasn't looking at *me*—she was looking at all my *clothing*. I wasn't dressed as a schoolgirl from Evanshire Academy.

I was dressed like the royal guest of a vampire lord.

It wasn't like I could come prepared when I was swept far away to another world. The only things I had on me at the time were my school uniform and a cell phone—one long lost and forgotten by now.

Elliott had his tailor outfit me in new clothes—well, his replacement one, after the first tried to suck my blood dry. Luckily, my vampire attire seemed to pass for the kinds of stuff that other human beings wore, even if it was a tad *eccentric* in the fashion department...

Then there was the amulet.

Gleaming in the dim light, the black amulet around my neck rested against my collarbone. Inset with a large red ruby, it was a visually striking piece of old jewelry that had appeared while I was on Elliott's world while trapped in a magical coma. I had seen this beautiful amulet on *this* world once before, long ago...

I was amazed she hadn't said anything about it.

"And you're wearing this," she continued, pointing to my clothes but still failing to mention the amulet. It was almost as if she didn't even *see* it. "This is the kind of thing I'd expect to see on a fashion runway, or maybe at a fancy dress dinner..."

The therapist blinked her eyes up to mine.

"You were sopping wet when they found you, but only from the waist down. That means that you weren't tossed into the lake to drown. Instead, you were found facedown at the edge of the water, abandoned."

I didn't respond.

"So, this is what I think happened."

Please, lady, I grumbled in my head. *Just let me go.*

"You were kidnapped, clearly. The clothing that you're wearing isn't something a girl in your position can afford, and there's nothing anywhere *near* here that sells that kind of material. Maybe you could find a dress like that down in London, but so far we've turned up nothing on CCTV during the time you were missing."

She referred, of course, to the blanket surveillance that covered the United Kingdom. It had never occurred to me that my disappearance would set off a nationwide search, or that they'd start checking the camera systems.

"For the moment, my colleagues and I are operating under the idea that you never strayed *far* from that park." She relaxed in her chair. "Feel free to confirm or deny..."

I remained silent.

"And there's something else..."

No, I realized to my horror. *Don't do it. Don't*—

"The caretaker who first found you. He stated that you rambled while he waited for the officers to pick you up..."

No. Don't say—

"Vampires," the therapist continued with a lifted brow. "When he asked you where you'd been, he says you told him you had been living in a castle filled with vampires. A castle underneath a sky where you could always see the stars, even during the day..." She nearly smirked. "And he tells us that you kept calling out a name..."

Without her realizing, she crushed my spirit.

"...Elliott." She looked at me. "Who is 'Elliott'?"

My gaze dropped hard to the tabletop in front. I could feel the tears welling behind my eyes. There just wasn't enough strength left in me to hold them back.

Who *wasn't* Elliott?

Handsome. Savvy. Practical. Gone forever.

Elliott Craven—the dark, conflicted vampire lord who ruled over a parallel world version of Europe. That man was my entire world. Forced into a seat of power he didn't want and surrounded by enemies, he desperately tried to keep his entire realm from tearing itself apart around him.

I **loved** him. And he...

He repaid my love by *sending me away*.

The therapist reached over and handed me a tissue to wipe my eyes. "Was Elliott the man who took you?"

My head shook subtly, even as I tried to stop it.

"Was he the man who brought you back to the park?" Now that my body had betrayed me with the slightest hint of a response, this woman was clearly determined to chase this topic to the grave. "Did Elliott help you escape from the place where you were taken?"

In a way, he did—against my wishes. But I couldn't

tell this woman the truth. Even if I trusted her, I knew that she would never believe me. *I mean, how **could** she?*

The therapist sighed, scooping her notepad back up off the table and relaxed into her chair. "There's another thing. The same driver who confirmed your route the morning of your disappearance told us you showed him some marks on your arm. You convinced him to let you on for free, and you claimed that it was..." She glanced down at her notes once again; I suspected the gesture was for show. "...The fault of your stepfather. That he's alcoholic." She paused for effect, studying me. "You implied he was abusive."

Confused, I sipped my tea.

I remembered these things, very faintly, but they felt so very far away now. After all I had been through these last few weeks... recalling something like a bus driver I'd seen, or some marks on my arm, took too much brainpower.

"Did your stepfather hurt you, Clara? We're prepared to make an arrest if you talk to us. He left a bad impression on the questioning officers. A very bad one."

I tried to process this. My exhausted brain struggled to wrap itself around what she was saying. Everything was so new to me, and I still felt numb and alone. I wished that I was anywhere else—even in the interrogation chamber down beneath Stonehold Castle.

Suddenly, I felt like I was there again.

The stainless steel table between us was now wood and stone. Instead of a suspicious older woman with a notepad and a pen, another person entirely sat across from me: the beautiful, pale arms of young Elliott Craven folded as he relaxed back into his chair. A smooth, handsome smirk hit his face as the candle between us flickered, fighting away the surrounding darkness.

Desperately, I tried to hold the picture in my head.

But I blinked—and I snapped back.

No vampire lords or castles. No impossible skies above. Just this dreary police room, this suspicious woman, and me.

The therapist didn't seem to notice how my heart broke inside me. "You tried to run away from your stepfather, and he caught up to you, didn't he? Wasn't that what you were doing on that bus in the first place? Running away? He then took you somewhere—it couldn't have been back home, we did a sweep of the house. We think he punished you for trying to escape. Did he get you those clothes? Did he tell you to wear them?"

I didn't reply. *Could they really—*

"Clara. You don't have to defend him here," she stated. I could see the anticipation lighting up her face. "He can't hurt you here. Not not. Tell us what happened, and we can make this man go away. We'll put you in a new home, a new city, even a new school. You'll be safe. You will never have to see him again."

Memories of Harold snapped back—the man who had been taking care of me for years, in the loosest definition of the phrase. My life had been hell under his 'care.' *That's the life that waits for me again now, isn't it? Struggling through the horrible nights and the worse weekends, tending to every whim, barely able to keep up with my schoolwork... which, I guess I'm a month behind now. There goes my chances at booking myself a decent uni for grad school...*

But the compulsion was strong. I could leave him—and the rest of this—all far behind. If I could just bring myself to reach out and *take* the opportunity at hand... I could free myself of his torment and *punish* him in one fell swoop.

Then I remembered a friendly face—with the name of someone nearly forgotten. Someone from my life before...

Peter.

"A new school?" I asked, confused.

"Yes. You can leave this all behind."

"No," I blurted out.

She was taken aback. "What?"

"No," I insisted. "Harold didn't take me."

The therapist's anticipation switched into exasperation. "You're *positive,* Clara? You're certain that your step-father really had *nothing* to do with any of this?"

For another dark, tempting moment...

Harold had brought my world such despair and pain.

Life was miserable with him still in it; in my fractured state of mind, this was my way to get rid of him forever… and didn't I *deserve* that? Didn't I *deserve* freedom from the proverbial cage he had locked me in?

Hadn't I *earned* that?

But… as evil as that man could be, he would *never* do the things this woman had imagined. He was innocent of this. Guilty of many other things, yes, but not this.

And then there was Peter.

I hadn't thought about Peter Tatham in weeks. He was there the day I was transported away, even if only by text. My best friend wanted to invite me to a school social. It was slowly coming back to me. Probably as a date, if other friends were to be believed—the cute, caring boy picked the worst possible day to try and finally play that card.

He knew my home life. Peter was my one real ally in this place. He knew things about me that nobody else did. Peter understood just how miserable my life was, and he'd tried to take care of me before. He had earned my trust.

To survive that world of fangs and blood, I'd needed to let go of my life before. I had to push Peter out of my head. But now that I was back I needed *someone* I could count on. Elliott had betrayed me; Peter was all I had left anymore.

The choice sat before me.

And so I chose the harder path.

"Harold wasn't involved," I told her with the heaviest of hearts, before I could think long enough to change my mind. "He wouldn't do something like that to me."

The therapist sighed as I sealed my fate.

CHAPTER 1

CLARA

TWO MONTHS LATER

W ithering trees and shadows surrounded me at every last turn. Each racing footstep pounded hard in my heart, like the beating of a war drum. I knew a dark and unsettling truth: the moment that my shoes stopped propelling me forward, I would be slain on the spot.

I knew this because I'd dreamt it.

*I'd dreamt it **over** and **over** again.*

This nightmare was not unfamiliar to me. I'd endured it for weeks before I came to Elliott's world—where it very mysteriously disappeared, until my final night there. And when I came back to my home world...

It returned. Worse than ever.

The recurring forest nightmare no longer came for me just at night. Any time I drifted off now, even during the daylight hours, it slipped back into my mind—

stealing away my rest. There was no denying it now. Whatever was happening to me, it was powered by nothing less than a violent and predatory vengeance.

At least, after so many sleepless nights since the dream came roaring back, the trauma finally rewarded me with a weapon. I'd grown lucid enough in my sleep to retain a certain sense of dream awareness. At long last, from inside the nightmare... I now knew that I was asleep.

And it changed... *nothing*.

At first, it had felt like such a powerful new revelation. When I finally realized that I was dreaming from within the nightmare, a sense of power and control swept away the looming terror. Confident in myself, and confident that I was now untouchable, I finally made a definitive change. I schemed to decisively take my dreams back into my own trembling hands.

For the first time since I'd ever endured this haunting nightmare, I stopped running. I turned back. I faced down the predatory force as I prepared to fend it off myself.

Or so I thought.

That very first death was the worst.

There really was no stopping the entity that stalked me in the dream forest. There was no pleading with it. Once it caught me, I died with a mouth screaming in terror and a soul wrenching with blind agony. The unspoken *thing* that so viciously pursued me did not even have the common decency to show itself. The most that I could ever make out was the silhouette of a powerful shape in the darkness. The *real* fear came not from its form but from the sheer, unending **hatred** that I felt pouring out of it.

By now, I'd had plenty of time to study the predator in all of its malevolence. I didn't know its face or its name, but I knew *it*. I knew that when the day came that I had to face it outside of my dreams, this creature would be no stranger to me at all. I'd recognize it for what it was—and I'd have only one sliver of a chance to succeed where I had so often failed.

Exhaustion settled in. Powered only by adrenaline, my ragged footsteps dragged me to the moonlit edge of the woods. Across a vast and violent sea was a distant island; every time I saw it, standing on the edge of this clifftop, it silently called to me. I knew that my salvation was on that island, somewhere.

If only I could actually **reach** *it...*

I knew the jump would kill me. From such a height, the water would be like concrete to my fragile bones; the wild waves writhed below, surely eager to shred my weak body alive against the jagged rocks in the surf.

There was a reason why I knew so strongly that I'd face this force in the real world. There was another part to this dream—another force that rose to combat it. The shadowy figure of a man was the only protection I had in this vile place. Within my nightmares, he was a powerful silhouette with a handsome voice and burning eyes.

And on a world barely removed from my own, after an impossible journey, I *met* him. *I **actually** met him.* Just as he was my protector in this nightmare, outside my dreams he was my guardian—protecting me from a dangerous world filled with bloodthirsty vampires, none of whom had ever *seen* a live human being before...

As this unnaturally formidable, conflicted man strived to save me from a world on the brink of warfare, I came to know him by his true name: Elliott Craven, the vampire lord of Stonehold. So mighty was my beloved Elliott that even his mere presence near me banished my bad dreams. While I rested in his company, I slept more peacefully than I had in a nearly a month. Struggle as it might, the recurring horror could not find me.

At least, until the night before he sent me away...

With the sheer cliff dive before me, my attention pulled to the trees. The vicious force in the forest roared forward, filled with unexplained malice. Knowing it would only be a matter of time before it reached me and destroyed me on the spot, I put my back to the swirling ocean and awaited the shadow of my handsome Elliott.

But I knew he wouldn't come.

He never did anymore.

Once I'd become lucid enough to fight back against

the nightmare, the dream itself changed. The shadow of Elliott no longer appeared from the woods to save my life. Even jumping from this cliff, as he'd always demanded before, didn't end the dream anymore. Now, every night when I fell asleep, every day when I drifted off, no matter what I ever did, I died.

And my deaths were soaked in terror and anguish.

The trees themselves quaked in fear as the unspeakable force reached me. I heard nothing but felt *everything* as the storm barreled down upon me, as it did so many times—

"MISS BLACKWELL?"

In a jolt, my head lifted from my desk.

Holding her retractable rod in her cupped fist, the teacher glared across from the dry erase board. "It's nice of you to join us again, Miss Blackwell... daresay, I do hope my class doesn't bore you *that* much. But I'm sure your adventures must have been *far* more exciting than this..."

Snickers rose near me as I sighed, rubbing the sleep from my eyes. My lethargic gaze drifted to the left—that was a mistake. Peter sat one row over and a few seats up, a look of wounded concern on his face. I rapidly turned away, unable to meet the questions in his stare.

I sat up straight. "I'm sorry."

She narrowed her eyes. "See that you *stay* sorry."

With that, I steeled myself in my chair.

For the next half of an hour, I faintly pretended to pay attention to her ambling lecture. *Come on, bell,* I silently prayed as I glanced at the clock. *Any moment now...*

Finally, it rang and we were dismissed.

"Don't you forget!" The teacher glared over us all as we cleared our desktops and rose from our chairs. "First exams are coming up first thing Monday! I don't want to hear any excuses; you have *all weekend* to be prepared!"

I trudged out into the hallway, pushed along in the crowd of excited students. It was finally the best part of the week—the end of school on a Friday afternoon.

"Hey!" I heard his voice. "Wait up!"

I don't have the energy for this, I moaned in my head.

"Hey, Peter," I turned to my friend. He trotted up to me with a concerned smile on his face. "What's up?"

"Not much," he shrugged. "Just a little worried about you back there, that's all. Did you have that dream again?" He leaned in closer. "How'd it go this time?"

I sighed. "It caught me at the cliff's edge."

"You ran," Peter nodded thoughtfully. He coolly ran a hand through his thick mop of curly brunette hair. The sunlight hit my best friend just the right way; it made his tanned skin look even more attractive than before.

"Good on you, Clara. One of these days, I know that you'll outrun it. You'll beat it. Maybe not now—but *soon*."

I felt bad. For years, I'd nursed a harmless crush on my best friend, ever since Harold moved us over to this part of town. It wasn't like Peter had ever been the love of my life or anything. Still, I had always found myself wondering what could happen—I mean, it wasn't hard to appreciate his natural confidence and handsomeness.

But by the time that he finally started showing signs of reciprocating, I'd been whisked away to another world and met someone extraordinary. *Could I ever forget that?*

"How do you feel about catching a movie tonight?" Peter asked slyly. "Just the two of us."

I paused. "I wish I could, but Harold..."

His cheery disposition didn't falter a step. "Maybe I can talk some sense into that man. I got to know him when you went missing. Your crusty old stepdad *finally* started to take to me, I guess. Kind of. I think."

I wasn't sure if I liked that.

"Peter..." I started to rebuke him.

"Not a date," he held his hands up in defense. "Trust me, I know. I won't try and put you through the ringer, Clara. I just want to know that you're okay."

Was *I okay?* I wasn't sure.

"Peter, you know better than anyone else what my stepfather's like—what he's *always* been like." My friend sped up to hold the door open for me, and I stepped out of our secondary school, Evanshire Academy. The refreshing sunlight hit my skin. After a week buried in schoolwork, it felt fantastic to be back outside again, even if only for a few minutes.

"Maybe I can change his mind," he shrugged.

I scowled, turning to pause us at the foot of the stairs. All of the other students flooded out around us like raging water, filled with laughter and relief. *All of you, so eager to meet your weekends—whereas for **me**…*

"He's punished me ever since I showed back up."

"Well, Clara…" Peter's lip curled into a half-frown. He glanced around us before leaning in quietly. "Maybe if you told him what *really* happened in the weeks while you went missing, he'd be a little, I don't know…"

"Lighter on me?" I narrowed my eyes.

"It's just a suggestion," he replied defensively.

"We both know that's impossible."

Peter sighed deeply. "Yeah. The psychologists all had their say." I felt his hand on my shoulder; my best friend lowered his face, searching my eyes. Quietly, I turned to avoid his gaze. "But I *know* you, Clara. There's a lot more to it, isn't there? Do you want to know what I think?"

"Sure," I rolled my eyes. "Fill me in."

He ignored my attitude. "I think that you *do* remember. I think you never really forgot—at least, it's still trapped in here, somewhere." He placed his fingertip to my forehead. "But all that crazy stuff you were saying when you were found—all about *vampires* and *other worlds* —I think it was some kind of fever dream. Just your overwhelmed brain struggling to process what *really* happened."

I pretended to listen.

I even pretended to care.

"It's like that thing with your necklace," Peter smiled in concern, watching how I fiddled aloofly with it. I hadn't even realized that I was doing it. "Remember how crazy you sounded when you showed it to me?"

"Yeah," I replied dejectedly.

Peter couldn't see the amulet for what it really was. It seemed that *nobody* could. To everybody else in the world, it was a simple silver necklace chain around my neck, not a dark and gorgeous black amulet.

I wondered why I was the only one to *really* see it.

"If you hadn't already told me about this nightmare of yours before you left, I guess I might've thought *that* was part of this all as well..."

Peter tenderly put his other hand on my shoulder too; had this been *before* I vanished, I might have even blushed at his touch. "I believe in you, Clara. I have a lot of faith in you. Someday, whenever you're ready, you can tell me the truth. Until then..."

He released his hands from me, shoving them both in the warm pockets of his academy blazer. "I will *always* be here for you, Clara. You know that."

I nodded quietly. "I do."

"Good. Now, don't fight me on this. Just let me have a word with Harold. Unless you'd rather stay trapped in that house with him—and I'll be honest here, that might hurt my feelings—I'll see if we can't get you out for a few hours." He smiled with that classic *Peter* grin of his, the one I'd seen for years. It was his way of showing that he cheerfully accepted all my flaws and adored me anyway, even if we were destined to be friends and nothing more.

And as we sat in a crowded cinema that night, while Peter Tatham slyly played off wrapping his arm around my shoulder, my mind couldn't help but drift away.

I *did* remember.

I remembered *everything*.

And that was what made it all hurt so much.

CHAPTER 2

ELLIOTT

From far atop Craven Keep, the highest point of the entire castle, I silently watched the first few flakes of snow. White dust trailed lightly against the crisp breeze of the open air, dancing around itself as it glided over the walled, tooth-like edge of the tower's rooftop. With mild interest, I followed its descent with my gaze.

Such fragile little things...

"It will be a cold year," I noted calmly.

Nikki Craven stepped into place at my side. Brushing strands of long, platinum blonde hair out from her face, my insanity-stricken sister looked over the darkening sky above the island. The vast, forested Isle of Obsidian stood as the seat of the Craven bloodline—and it held the royal, ancient stone castle that was our birthright.

Well, thanks to her latest actions, *my* birthright.

"Never a good sign when the snowfall comes this early in the season. The people always said the kingdom reflects the heart of its master." I hid a sigh; she turned to me with a dark and cunning gaze. "And *your* heart is the coldest in the hold. It comes as little surprise that our wild Stonehold suffers the turmoil of its sitting lord..."

I let my silence serve as a reply.

"You know, brother dearest..."

"Don't," I ordered.

She cheerfully ignored me. "You seem rather foul in the mood department today, even more than the usual. What's gotten *your* fangs caught up in a twist?" Nikki leaned a little forward, peering into my eyes with a wicked grin.

Nearly any other vampire on the planet would have shuddered at the death glare I gave her. Naturally, Nikki laughed at such notions. While I didn't *precisely* know what went on in that twisted, demented little head of hers, my personal impression was that Nikki battled demons I'd never equal—even at my very worst.

Even Kinsey cleared her throat uncomfortably.

Beyond my sister, Kinsey was the only other vampire I allowed in my presence atop the keep. She'd all but sworn to follow me to the grave. Hell, she very nearly had. She was willing to give the ultimate sacrifice in a nightmarish mining cavern, taking a blow from a living embodiment of death that meant to kill me. The resulting damage left the young royal guard, a prodigy in all but name, hospitalized for weeks.

Such reasons were why I made Kinsey my vassal—my sworn guardian, near-constant companion, and an advisor. My mother might have seen fit to abolish the system, but I was an unworthy successor and everyone knew it—not for a lack of trying. To be personally appointed a vassal to the crown was the very highest honour for a living vampire.

"Well?" Nikki asked expectantly. "Why are you so—"

"Two months," I answered coolly. "To the day."

Her evil smile twitched. "Oh."

"Yes." Habitually, I folded my arms in frustration—the most common emotion that I found myself enduring in these trying times. Well, that wasn't *technically* true. Most of the time, the feeling was a pervasive numbness, soaking down into my very bones. "*Oh* is right."

I drew myself back into my memories.

THE COUNCIL OF THE EIGHT HOLDS—THE COLLECTIVE of the vampire lords who ruled our world with an iron fist—was lit with a chorus of fury.

And wouldn't they be? I'd just betrayed them all.

Out of all the other lords in their self-righteous anger,

it was my darkest enemy—the ancient, gnarled ruler of the Falvian Badlands—who kept my attention. Of what little I could prove, I knew the truth about Akachi Azuzi: he had already attempted to make a power grab for the fate of the human Clara Blackwell not once, but twice.

Both came with disastrous consequences.

First, his sudden appearance in my castle rattled me enough to try unproven magic that dropped the poor girl deep into a comatose state. It ultimately came to be for the best; Clara was no longer a target of every last blood-thirsty vampire on my staff. But her short, fragile life had hung in the balance while I was forced away, reconciling threats to my own people.

But it was the twisted plot of his agent in my midst—a threat that I'd equally failed to see coming, one who in the end betrayed even her own master—that finally convinced me I could not truly protect Clara Blackwell.

Thus, I found a way to send her back to her world.

But every move I made was another failure, no matter my best intentions. Every decision I made only succeeded in worsening the darkening path ahead.

I'd been so blind. So stupid.

The vampire lords had *all* felt the otherworldly arrival of the first human in recorded history—an alluring and frail creature, plucked straight out from our oldest stories. No matter how distant my opponents, all seated on their mighty thrones in their mighty castles, they had known in an instant that Clara had come.

They *knew* the moment that it happened.

It made perfect sense then, in retrospect, that my foes might feel the human's equally supernatural *departure*...

Mattias Blackburn called order to the council. Even the impartial ruler of the frozen and haunted Bleakwood —or "Canada" as Clara's world apparently called it— failed to hide his animosity. Built as the tallest and broadest among us, he followed the examples set by every other lord in the room and narrowed his eyes upon me.

"Explain," Mattias growled.

"I warned you that this could happen," I replied with my cool, controlled tone. My eyes scanned the other faces. "I warned you *all* that this could happen. The human girl arrived out of thin air! There was nothing to stop her from disappearing the same way."

"Lies," Akachi Azuzi snarled with blatant menace.

"Speak carefully," I warned, aware that only magical barriers separated our thrones from one another. If not for that protection, the most senior vampire lord in our midst would be free—personally inclined, even—to demonstrate just how his gnarled fingers had clung to his throne across centuries of countless mutinies and back-stabbing. I looked at him with a heavy yet nonconfrontational gaze. "Allow me to remind you not accuse anything you're unwilling to back up with proper evidence."

"Probable cause?" he glowered. "You made it painfully clear when we last met that you, young Lord Craven, had no desire to relinquish your little pet for the good of us all. And now, before we can make you see sense, you *banish* her away from this world!"

The others jeered in unison.

My eyes met those of Mattias. He was the only one of us whom we all trusted—the closest thing to a leader that we had. Always the mediator, always the voice of reason, there was nothing in that steeled gaze now to make him an ally, let alone any friend of mine. I was on my own here.

Unsurprised yet disappointed, I turned to the elderly lord. "How would you suggest that is possible?"

Azuzi's lip curled into a snarl. He wasn't sure.

"This might be of relevance," the enigmatic, beautiful Svetlana Lovrić spoke up, ignoring my stare. "There was a peculiar... instance. Our instruments noticed some sort of catastrophic disturbance, late the evening in question. My scientists were at a loss at the time, but..." The ruler of the Drenchlands turned to face me with a curt smile. Her mysterious domain beneath the sea was the uncontested seat of scientific advancement in our world; we all knew it. "This is different from the first time. They did not react in such a way when Clara Blackwell first arrived. What, then, could have caused them such distress?"

Even if she was just as antagonistic as the others, I took note of her civility. *At least **she** refers to Clara by name...*

"I don't know," I answered obliquely.

"You... You don't know?" She blinked in annoyance.

"Perhaps if your instruments were on *her* world when she first left it, they would have registered the same thing. I do not know how this happened—just like I have no idea how she first arrived here. If these precious instruments of yours have happened to solve *that* particular mystery..." My face matched her annoyance. "Please, do *tell*."

Svetlana swallowed angrily, but said nothing.

She was among the far more reasonable vampire lords. It wasn't wise for me to combat her like this— especially after I had incidentally mocked her the last time we met. With that said, that innocent little observation of hers had backed me into *quite* the corner...

"I wish to see those readings," Mattias replied. "There could be a way to bring her back here." He glanced at me with a knowing look. "Although, it seems to me now that perhaps you would *dislike* that outcome, Lord Craven."

If my skin could have paled any further...

The others searched my expression. Foolishly, I hadn't thought to feign remorse at Clara's sudden disappearance. The wounds were still fresh, and I suffered from them. But hardening my heart in the face of great personal tragedy had left me bitter and combative. The others would begin to question that—and it would lend support to the theory that I'd banished her *myself*...

"Being around the human is complicated," I bluffed a confession, pretending to believe my own words. "She and I were such fundamentally different creatures that it could be difficult to understand her. We bickered endlessly." As I noticed the curious looks on their faces, I lied even harder. "From an outsider's perspective, she stayed at my *throat*... metaphorically speaking. Her presence here brought pain and the potential for ruin. Forgive me then, my lords, if I find that I'm not destroyed by her sudden absence."

"Are you admitting then that you would willingly give her up?" Valentine Vasiliev leaned forward curiously, her sinister smile filling me with dread. If there was one lord on this council that I'd fear getting their hands on Clara over even Akachi Azuzi, it was the ruler of The Wastes. "Because I was under the impression, as many of us were, that you felt rather *differently* last time we all met..."

I hesitated. *What does it really matter now? She's gone.*

In another hundred years, Clara Blackwell would be long dead and buried on her own world, lost forever. I'd never see her again—and my priority now was to prevent an escalating global war between vampires.

There was only one right answer to this question.

"If she returns, you're welcome to her," I snarled.

The other lords murmured among themselves. Mattias tried in vain to silence them and to bring order back to the Council of the Eight Holds; they were all *understandably* surprised by my answer.

Akachi Azuzi was the only lord who remained silent.

Carefully, the haggard old vampire watched my face, stroking his long, white beard from his ebony-black flesh. I maintained eye contact with him for a fleeting moment as something unspoken passed between us; his face grinned with defeat. *You understand, then. Good. You've overplayed your hand—and lost your single, tantalizing chance for the most ambitious power grab in recorded history...*

*It is enough for me to lose, Akachi. So long as **you** fail.*

Satisfied with a stalemate, I leaned back in my chair.

Clara Blackwell... I banished her away from my realm to protect her. I'd told her, the moment we met, that her very presence in this world shoved it to the utter brink of chaos. In my haste to protect her, it seemed I'd moved the tipping point straight to my own throne...

MY MEMORIES FADED WHEN I NOTICED HOW NIKKI

looked at me, biting her bottom lip with a fang to the point of drawing blood. Kinsey pretended to not pay attention.

"Elliott, she's not coming back."

"I know," I snapped darkly. "We were there."

The lingering hint of a rebuttal hung in the back of her throat. I turned away, giving her the opportunity to hit me with one of her infamously sarcastic responses. At the last second, she instead swallowed it.

"You have been manageable lately," I observed calmly. "None of your usual mood swings. You've even stopped threatening to butcher the subjects of this castle."

Nikki smirked to herself. "I'd better fix that, then."

"As conventional wisdom seems to dictate, it's forever the *quiet* ones someone must watch out for. Then again, the ones who wrote the conventional wisdom never met *you*."

Her head tilted. "Are you calling me *loud?*"

"I'm calling you *openly malicious*."

"Fair point."

We stood in silence together like that for a moment. It was peaceful to be near her—despite the atrocities she had committed on this island and likely countless others in her exile. I still had complex feelings towards my sister, given our history together—especially our more *recent* history.

But for all her faults, she was the only family I had left. *And nothing's thicker than blood.*

"Kinsey... how long has Lorelei been gone?"

My vassal thought about that for a second. "Didn't you say that Clara's been gone two months today, to the day?"

"That's right."

"Then two months. Minus a day."

I scowled, turning to my sister. "Any leads?"

She shrugged. "Nope. Mum's done a runner. As far as I can tell, she's disappeared off the face of the planet. Given what we've all been through recently, I guess I wouldn't be too surprised..."

Typical. I expected nothing less from her.

"So," she added, "unless you *need* me..."

I smiled. Of course she had to ask me permission, or at least feign the gesture. Nikki was now *also* my vassal.

Her heart had been in the right place—probably—but she had still betrayed me and, by extension, the crown. In my fury, I had stripped my sister of her birthright; she lost her blood claim to a throne she clearly never even wanted. But in my mercy, I turned around in the same breath and made her my guardian and companion—my first vassal, an appointment set even before I lifted Kinsey to the title.

"No," I decided. "You may leave."

Nikki hopped up onto the tower's battlement, ready

EMMA GLASS

to drop down Craven Keep safely to the ground far
below. Of course, it would have made far more sense to
simply take the chrysm node in the keep wherever she
wanted to go—and it probably would have startled my
subjects a lot less. But that had not been my sister's way,
not in a long time.

Before she could make her dramatic little exit from
my company, I halted her with a question. "Have you
forgiven me yet? For what we did to Clara?"

As I had before, she let her silence serve as a reply.

And then she was gone.

CHAPTER 3
CLARA

The weeks meant nothing to me.

They all blended together like creeks pouring into a river, with no real difference from one week to the next. I was just a leaf on the water. I was there for the ride, left to swirl around in the ripples and waves with no control of my own.

And I barely cared.

That's not to say that I didn't try.

Put yourself in my shoes, and you might understand.

Let's pretend that—*right this very moment*—you live a horrible life, ruled by a horrible person. But now, you find yourself tugged far away to some magical and impossibly wonderful place. This place is so fascinating and amazing that it convinces you to leave behind all you valued. Your entire place in the world comes to a screeching halt; all of your carefully laid plans for the future go up in smoke with the click of your fingers.

Really. Picture it, just for a moment.

Picture that the entire dynamic of your life is rewritten. Every fundamental piece of importance you've given to all the tiny little details of your life, in a heartbeat, instantly mean *nothing*—and you realize that it's the best thing that ever happened to you. You're shown this incredible place that redefines the very essence of happiness...

And then... *you're ripped back*.

You're thrown into that horrible life again.

You've tasted passion, and now you've been *denied* it.

I was sixteen years old when I was first thrust between worlds. There was nothing that could have prepared me for the dangers I faced or the beauty I beheld. Nothing in this life could have made my mind ready for it all.

When I came back, I was seventeen.

In that tiny slice of my life, everything had changed.

So much had happened to me—so much danger and so much wonder. As quickly as it was mine, I was hurled once again into my dreary old life, dropped back into the West Midlands of England—and, worse still, I knew that *nobody* would ever believe me.

I was truly and unimaginably alone.

And now, months had passed since I first re-awakened, disoriented and terrified on the edge of the lake that sent me there in the first place. I had to convince myself that I could accept this old life back, or else I knew I'd be driven mad. I had to *try* to accept it.

So, I found solace in a diary, picked from a store.

The basic idea was simple enough: keep track of all my days and jot down my thoughts on daily life. But after two weeks of scribbling in the margins, I eventually took down the diary and flipped through the pages with fresh eyes.

They were all the same.

The pages were filled with emptiness and lies.

I decided to just leave it alone until something came up that was thrilling enough for me to remember. It remained a promise to myself—a promise to keep watch now for the beautiful and the exceptional in my life, and to write these things down and preserve them forever.

At some point after that, I forgot I had the diary at all. It collected dust in its drawer. Just like every other nearly empty book out there, it sat in its designated spot —filled with all the potential of the world.

Waiting.

I TOLD HAROLD THAT I WAS DOING HOMEWORK LONG hours after school in a study session. As far as he was concerned, it spared him having to pick me up from school.

As long as I found myself a way back home, he'd never be any the wiser.

Instead of burying myself in the library, I took the long bus ride over to the peaceful, old Midlands town where I first found Broadmoor Park and its splendorous lake, lost behind rampant overgrowth and broken paths.

It wasn't the first time I'd been back. It hadn't been as often as I would have liked—Harold saw to it that I had as little free time as he could possibly manage.

But it was often enough.

I stepped through the rusted gate, amused that the sign was still held together with the ribbon I'd loaned it.

"Good to see you again," I greeted it.

Being a ribbon, it didn't have much to say.

Beyond the gate, I was transported back to a time that was mostly untouched by human interference.

Mother Nature in her ceaseless patience had long since reclaimed this place. Branches far above formed a canopy that drowned it all in darkness. The entire park was buried beneath out-of-control underbrush and scattered branches or twigs; the pavement paths spread into the dark in ruin, gnarled and broken by the rising of powerful tree roots.

This lost domain became kindred to me as I walked its winding paths. It was only on my third visit back here that I realized something: I'd never seen the slightest activity of life. Nothing stirred in the bushes; no sounds of distant birds or breaking twigs ever hit my ears.

The park did not strike me as ominous.

Still... it seemed out of place in this world.

I knew the way. Twenty minutes of walking, and I soon happened across the familiar, welcoming sight of the quiet and abandoned Broadmoor Park lake.

I made a point to try and reach it as often as possible, even with the hurdles Harold forced into my life. Most of the time, I had to skip a week or two between visits, but I still kept coming back.

I can't explain why I kept doing it.

Maybe I just hoped, or even *prayed,* that this silent lake would whisk me back into the arms of Elliott Craven.

Of course, that would never happen.

The lake stood surrounded by thick, untamed grass on all sides. Only the continuing pavement that blazed a trail through the unkempt wilderness here offered any sort of guiding path, and even they stood cracked and torn apart by the underlying roots.

I walked up the path to the wooden dock.

The first time I'd ever been here, there was another. She was an ancient, gnarled gypsy woman—a decrepit old hag whose eyes came in two different colours. Her rotten teeth begat breath that smelled of death, and her filthy robes looked to be torn from a buried coffin.

She had known my name.

She'd blamed me for... *something*.

The gypsy woman chased me towards the lake, and I'd run for my life. She'd reminded me of the creature in my nightmares—I took a page from Elliott's commands in my dream (back when he was still there, at least) and I bolted into the water.

That water sent me flying between worlds.

I'd utterly embarrassed myself the first time that I tried to repeat that performance, in my desperation to find my way into that terrifying but beautiful realm again.

I leapt into the cold water time and time again, hoping against logic that I'd be thrown back through an explosion of sights and colours, barreling through endless universes—until I woke up cold and alone, on the floor of an ancient castle in a dark and mystical world...

And later, I'd climbed back onto the bus sopping wet and stinking of lake water, trying to figure out what the hell I was supposed to tell Harold when he saw me.

It was a lucky day. He had passed out in his chair.

But I learned to never make that mistake again. I came here now prepared with a change of clothes in a backpack. There was no need to ruin my academy attire when a few local thrift stores carried second-hand towels and cheap spare clothes that I could destroy anew, time after time.

I climbed up onto the wooden dock and checked to see if the gypsy woman was back. She never was. I walked all the way down to the very end, even though I could see the distant tip of the bridge from the top step to the platform.

She was nowhere to be found. Again.

When I wandered back, I ducked around the corner of the steps and changed into my spare clothes. Walking out towards the shore and picking a decent spot, I re-imagined the blind panic that I had felt that fateful day. Retracing each step from that day, I launched into a sprint along the edge of the quietly lapping water.

My footfall turned at the last second.

I took a few strides and leapt over the grasses...

The freezing, muddy lake splashed up around me as I sank shin-deep into the muddy silt. My mouth filled with lake water and I spat out the bile.

Annoyed but not surprised, I plucked myself up and waded back to the shore. Climbing out from the lake and back onto the grassy shore, I lay down in the fluffy, spongy weeds. I stared up at the waning sunlight, as I had so often done in the last few months.

And, just like all those times...

I began to sob.

CHAPTER 4
CLARA

Peter was sick for a week.

He'd spent the entire weekend with his parents on a planned trip to Spain, but it sounded like they had all come back with a terrible souvenir: stomach flu.

"Are you sure you're okay?" I asked over the phone.

"Of course!" He chuckled weakly. His usually strong voice came down the line in a thin rasp. I hadn't heard him like that in years. "You're taking notes for me in Math and Biology. I've got Sam grabbing me a copy of what I need for English, and Packer's already got me covered in all the rest. Honestly, I'll be fine."

"You're certain?" I fretted, biting my lower lip. I didn't like him laid up in bed, even if he still had two seasons of the latest Netflix stuff to catch, plus a stack of video games he'd been itching to get around to.

EMMA GLASS

"Heh. Clara, if I didn't know any better, I might say that you almost sounded *concerned*..."

I smirked. "No idea where you got *that* idea from."

"Crazy, I know."

When our chuckling subsided, Peter and I settled into a comfortable silence. I loved how we didn't have to ever fill the void with talking. It's one of the things that I valued so much in our friendship—from experience, it's rare to find someone you can just coexist with, without the need to feel like you have to constantly impress.

I really valued that with him.

His voice came tentatively. "Listen, Clara..."

My stomach dropped. "Yeah?"

"After I've gotten better, how would you feel about, I dunno, maybe taking another stab at a movie night?

I swallowed. "Oh. Uh..."

The silence grew uncomfortable for a moment.

"You know what? Let me ask you this in person," Peter chuckled with the slightest tinge of nervousness. "I'm sure it'd sound *way* sexier if I wasn't tossing my guts up when I tried to rope you into that..."

I wanted to throw him *something*.

"I'll, um. I'll think about it."

"Cool," he answered. "Now then... if you'll excuse me, I've got a platoon of deadly alien marauders to beat down. They don't exactly punch themselves in the face.

They're real tossers like that... oh, that is the *ugliest* looking—"

"Wait. Peter, are you telling me you were gaming the *whole time* we've been on the phone?"

In the background, the telltale sounds of arcade gunfire came down the line; when I listened closer, I realized that he frantically smacked his joysticks. Peter grunted a cheery reply: "Clara Blackwell... I can neither confirm nor deny that horribly *wild* accusation."

"Yeah, yeah," I rolled my eyes as I disconnected.

Not seeing him in my classes all week underlined how much I needed him. Even if he didn't believe the truth—and even if I couldn't tell him the rest, knowing just how he'd react to what would admittedly sound pretty crazy—Peter had been my rock for months now.

He took care of me. He was the only one to make an effort to keep me uplifted and focused on the positives. Peter understood my complicated home life situation to an extent—enough that he knew how difficult it was for me to get any meaningful time away from the house.

Yet, I still kept him at arm's length.

Why? Doesn't he deserve something more?

What *more* meant, I didn't know.

But I wanted to make a bigger effort for him. I knew it couldn't be easy to deal with me, even if I understood that he didn't truly get why I was so miserable.

It was cruel for me to let him think that I'd been

abused or hurt while I was missing, but what else could I honestly do but let him draw that conclusion?

What's the right thing to do?

HE WAS BACK IN SCHOOL A FEW DAYS LATER. I couldn't tell if the pale skin was from his illness, or how long he spent indoors in front of his television.

It reminded me of a certain *somebody*...

But only pain paved that way down memory lane.

Peter plunked himself down next to me as I sat alone in the cafeteria, buried in thought. He smirked. "Oh man. It's so great to finally be able to eat solid food again! What've they got for today?"

"Don't hold your breath."

"Huh?" After a quick glance down at my lunch tray, his face contorted into a thwarted frown. "*Seriously?*"

"Enjoy what passes for beef stew." I took a bite.

Peter grumbled, venturing off for a couple of minutes; I watched him stand in line for lunch. He bumped into a couple classmates. Soon they were all laughing together.

Classic Peter, I thought. *Friends everywhere...*

Pensively, I sipped soup as I watched him interacting with them. Between his handsome looks and the cheery way he greeted people, being a fairly popular extrovert always came naturally to Peter Tatham.

I wonder if I could have ever been like that, I thought.

It seemed unreasonable to think such a thing possible now. After all, I'd spent my entire time back locked within the deep, harrowing depths of loss and sorrow. My heart felt so empty and meaningless. As much as I'd have loved to be proven wrong, there just wasn't anything that I could do to fix me—and, try as he might, handsome Peter was even less likely to find a way.

Speaking of, he plopped his tray down next to me with a huge grin. It soured when he spared another look at his lunch. His friends had been a distraction, but it was clear that his optimism had peaked. "Was solid food *honestly* too much to ask for?"

I shrugged, swallowing a bite. "Guess so. You must've really ticked off some sort of higher power there with all of that alien-smashing of yours. Looks like the galactic gods have forsaken you."

He chuckled. "Those aliens know what they did."

"Even so, Mr. Tatham, I'm afraid you picked the wrong week to miss. It was even taco day yesterday."

"Taco day?" He threw his hands up in disgust. "There was a bloody *taco day* yesterday? How often does *that* even come back around?"

"Never." I took another slurp of my stew.

"That's right. *Never.*"

"Not all of us can spend a week at home, passed out in front of the telly." I scooped the all-but-obligatory excuse for Italian bread down into the bowl. It wasn't half bad; I'd put it a tad closer to *three-quarters* bad, maybe. "Defending the Earth from all those bloodthirsty alien warriors."

Peter laughed, taking a bite of bread. "I was *very* sick."

"Is that right?"

"Oh yes," he nodded. "Wrecked, even."

"Yeah, yeah..." I rolled my eyes. "Anyway... it's good to have you back. I missed you."

"Good to *be* back."

"You're lying."

"Oh yeah. I'm definitely lying," Peter smirked. "Even if I was sick as a dog, that was one of the best weeks of my life. Hell, I begged my parents to take me back to Spain so we could do it all over again..."

"I take it they weren't too keen on that?"

"Apparently not." He swallowed a mouthful of broth; the expression on his face conceded he wasn't too torn up over it anymore.

I let the silence settle back in. I was rapidly running out of the energy for banter like this. The creeping sense of spiraling sadness—now all too familiar to me—began to sneak up in the back of my head, and I was resolute to get through this first lunch with him again before I had to excuse myself to cry in the bathroom.

"Hey," he looked over at me. "Are you alright?"

"Yeah," I lied. "Just distracted."

"Distracted?"

Alarmed, I dug around in my head for something to throw him off the scent. "Yeah. There's that quiz coming up in biology. I just haven't been sleeping well lately, so I can't focus on it all that well."

He nodded sympathetically. "The forest dream."

I could've kicked myself for giving him such a perfect backdoor to bring it up. "It's been better lately."

"Has it?" He raised an eyebrow.

"It's been... manageable."

"You're still dying every night, right?"

I sighed. "Yeah, I guess so."

"Doesn't sound all that manageable to me."

"You get used to it after a while."

I disappeared back into the beef stew. The last thing I wanted to do was get into a fight with him on our first day together again. But there was no persuading him to lay off this topic—or anything else related to the secrets I now felt like I had to keep from him.

"You look like you could use a distraction."

"Tell me about it," I groaned.

"Well..." Peter grinned sheepishly. "How about maybe that movie night, then?"

I had nearly forgotten about that.

Two for two. I actually kicked myself that time.

I made the mistake of looking at him—he was grinning at me like a dog awaiting a treat. *Meet him halfway. Peter's been looking out for you ever since you've gotten back— and don't forget, before you left, you were **thrilled** with even the idea of spending time with him like that. Besides, it's not as if you can go ever back to that castle.*

***That** chapter on your life is long gone...*

"Uh, alright then," I heard myself reply.

"Awesome. You want to go tonight?"

"*Tonight?*" I bit my lip broodingly. "That's too short of notice. I don't know if I can clear that with Harold."

"Well, if you can't, then we can work something out for later in the week." Peter offered casually as he dug around in his stew. "Or I can try and talk to him again."

"You can try..." I chuckled.

To my surprise, that's exactly what happened.

❧

UNDER A COLD AND OVERCAST SKY, I CLIMBED OFF THE bus and pulled my jacket tighter against the wind chill.

I remembered a time long back when I positively *loved* this weather. When I was still a young girl, there were few things I enjoyed more than the cold, breezy winds under a grey skyline—right before a storm. But now, that dark sky only reminded me of what I could no longer have: namely, a beautiful sky in a place far away from here.

No. I pushed the memories back down.

The bus stop was at the edge of the cinema parking lot. It wasn't long before I spotted Peter Tatham's thick, curly brunette hair on the edge of the crowd. I walked up to the boy, shoving my freezing hands in the front pockets of my hoodie. "Hey there."

"You made it!" His eyes lit up, showing me just how excited he really was that I'd shown up.

"*Of course* I made it," I shrugged apathetically.

"Cool. Are you ready to get your spook on?"

Oh no. "You didn't pick a scary one, did you?"

"What? No, no, of course I didn't," Peter rolled his eyes with a chuckle—he *definitely* picked a horror flick. "Why do you think I'd do something like that?"

"You *know* that I hate scary movies." Distraught, my lips thinned into a frown as I shook my head. "Can't we go see something else? *Anything* else?"

"Could, yeah, but I've already got tickets," he smirked, his eyebrow raised. I felt a twinge in my stomach, realizing how handsome he looked as he teased me. "Let's give it a shot, at least. People say you should fight fire with fire, right? Maybe it'll help out with the dreams. And hey—if you really don't like it, I'll pick something else. Deal?"

"Alright. Fine," I conceded. "What's it called?"

"*Blood Moon.* All the reviews make it sound like it's the best horror film to come out in a couple of years."

"If it gets us out of the cold, sure."

Peter led me up through the cinema doors, effortlessly cutting through the throng of people and marching us straight to the concessions counter. Following close behind him, I trailed in the wake he carved across the crowd.

"The usual?" He looked over his shoulder at me.

"We've only done this once," I reminded him.

My best friend chuckled. "The usual, then."

Even with my apprehension, it was difficult to not find Peter endearing. *How you're still single, I have no idea...*

So, I asked him. "Why are you single?"

"Why're you asking?" Peter grinned meaningfully.

"Just curious, I guess."

He thought for a moment. It seemed like he made a decision about something in his head, because the look he gave me seemed significant somehow.

"Well, that's probably because I—"

"Next!"

Peter blinked, realizing it was our turn.

"What did you want?" He asked hastily.

"I'm broke. You're already getting the movie."

"Nonsense. Can't do a film without the snacks!"

"I'm alright, really."

"I insist—"

The cashier repeated, snappily this time: "*Next!*"

Peter darted forward, leaning on the counter with a

sly, handsome smirk. *Classic Peter.* As he turned on the charm for the disgruntled worker, I pulled away from the throng of customers and hung over to the side, out of the way.

Distantly, I played with the amulet that rested against my collarbone. The pressure against my skin reassured me; I loved the weight of the thing, even if it struck me as odd that only I could see it for what it really was.

All else slowly faded away as I lightly fumbled with it. The world steadily grew quieter. The nearby commotion of moviegoers became steadily less important to me; I found myself embracing the mounting silence now. Zoning out, the surrounding quiet blanketed me in a sense of comfort and mild serenity. Even the light in the room itself seemed to darken with the passing seconds.

The carpet beneath my worn sneakers, I noticed, was a funny green colour. It struck me as kind of odd that they'd pick that shade—as if trying to put nature back in the...

Wait.

I realized in sudden horror that it wasn't carpet. What I was staring at was the floor of a forest—when I looked up, the people were gone, the cinema was gone, *everything else* was gone, all replaced with darkening, menacing trees that grew more vivid as the clock ticked onward.

In the distance, a horrible sound rose.

No, I gasped. *Not here too, not now*—

"Clara?"

I blinked, turning back to Peter. He stood before me, valiantly holding a large popcorn bucket in the crook of an arm with a pair of sodas in his hands.

"You okay? You seemed really out of it."

"Oh. Uh. Yeah," I nodded. "Of course I'm okay."

Peter scrutinized my expression for a moment, his face darkening; I clammed up on the inside.

"Are we doing this movie or not?" I finally asked.

Seemingly satisfied, he nodded, reaching out one of the large sodas. "Yeah. Here, take one of these and come on, then." After I did as he asked, he nodded over to the ticket usher with a small grin. I followed him over, but my head was already elsewhere.

The forest had seemed so *vivid.*

I'd never seen it outside of my dreams—waking or not. Nothing about seeing those woods here, staring into space, gave me less than a wave of crippling dread to the gut...

CHAPTER 5

ELLIOTT

As time passed and early winter descended upon the Isle of Obsidian, the nights grew ever colder and darker. The chill was bitter and relentless. It pervaded the entirety of my beloved Stonehold Castle, sucking the joy from everything it touched.

From my private balcony far atop Craven Keep—the tallest tower in the castle—I watched the courtyards. The only visible activity these days sequestered itself around a few roaring bonfires. The subjects of my castle cavorted in the open air with swapped tales and partying song near the blazes—careful to not get too close and with buckets of anti-freeze water at hand, just in case.

I envied them.

I didn't see what there was to celebrate.

The sound of my sister's pounding footsteps hit my ear before I saw her. I heard her run up the side of the tower to overtake my balcony; sliding down the cobble-stones above in a graceful stance, she landed near my side, rising to her feet in a swoop of her cloak.

"Elliott."

I flattened my palms against the frigid stone railing as I bent forward. "Why do they dance and sing?"

Nikki turned to follow my gaze.

"It isn't like there's anything better to do here, really," she answered with a shrug. "The sunlight wanes. Another few months—maybe even less—and it'll all be gone. Been a long time since a winter has taken away all the sun from Stonehold. Now's as good a time as any to enjoy it."

I glowered. "It's stupid."

"What might you have them do instead?" She replied coolly. "Stay indoors for months at a time? Unwilling to step out into the dusk, to be among their friends?"

My eyes rolled. "Here we go."

"If you're expecting a lecture, forget it."

"How noble of you."

"I honestly couldn't care less if you spent the rest of the winter locked away up in this tower," Nikki shrugged. "At least you're safe here with your own private statue."

She turned over her shoulder to gaze into my suite. Kinsey sat motionlessly at the dining table, asleep with her eyes wide open. The anatomy special to the brains of the royal guards gave them the capability of bringing all their basic functions to a halt. They were frozen in time... until they were needed, at least.

It was not an innate biological function. Bestowing that ability required certain... *modification*. I didn't know all the details. Among the myriad things the preceding lord failed to convey before suddenly handing off the throne, this was yet another. But it didn't sound pleasant.

"Speaking of," Nikki continued, staring at my other vassal, "how long's she been playing this entertaining little game of freeze tag?"

"Since yesterday."

"Maybe I wasn't specific enough." Nikki cupped her elbow, pinching the bridge of her nose. "Elliott, how long has it been since she's been awake for longer than, I don't know..." She lifted her gaze to me with an annoyed look. "Thirty seconds, maybe?"

I tilted my head. "Since the rest of the accompanying guards still in our medical bay were formally released. She wanted to congratulate them all on their survival."

Nikki scoffed. "Elliott, that was *three months* ago."

"Was it now?" I couldn't properly place it in my head. The days were all a blur to me. "By this point, I expected the vampire lords to have struck Stonehold."

"Almost a disappointment, yes..." Nikki's eyes lit up at the thought of the wanton bloodshed. I couldn't even imagine how much my little sister enjoyed the thought of pure carnage, even if her entire reason for leaving behind her self-imposed exile was to warn me of the coming war. I similarly couldn't fathom how difficult it must have been for her. *Always reconciling these warring sides of your mind...* But, these days, I found I just really didn't care anymore. "They've been quiet lately, that's for certain."

"I'd be more suspicious, if not for Silas."

"Oh?" She looked at me curiously.

"Yes. The old windbag tells me that the other holds are dealing with small catastrophes of their own. I imagine it's the entire reason there hasn't been another assembly of the council." Glancing lazily over the horizon again, I allowed my bored tone to convey my complete lack of interest. "I suppose I've been gifted some much-needed time."

She piqued up. "What *kinds* of catastrophes?"

"The world erupts into chaos abroad," I told her coolly. "The Falvian Badlands is undergoing a drought that has stirred the wildlife into a craze. Bleakwood is running out of food—and the vampires that far north are struggling to adapt to the chilling gales. Hexes have been spreading in Alevorra and Selvara Karn; they've been preoccupied with containing the magical contamina-tions." My eyes scoured the horizon, gazing over the forests that surrounded the castle. "Nobody's heard anything from the Drenchlands in a while—there's no telling what's going on down there."

"So, the other vampire lords...?"

"Distracted, yes." I noted matter-of-factly. "They're all so tied up in their own problems, they can barely spare the time to consider a mounted strike against us. Convenient, but it won't last forever, I suppose. Unless it does—and by then, the world will have ripped itself apart for us. No need for a war when the realm is handling that for itself."

I was interrupted by an elderly voice I despised.

"So you *have* been paying attention, then."

Nikki and I turned to greet my high chancellor Silas, strolling across my suite. Kinsey had already snapped to alertness, rising from her table to confront him.

"You know the rules," she warned him.

"Yes, yes, of course," he waved her away. "*Nobody on the castle grounds may step foot in the royal suite—not without the express permission of the sitting vampire lord.* You will find, young one, that I'm more than aware of the rules. I was there when many of them were **written**."

"This had better be good," I interjected darkly.

Silas sighed. "My Lord, you have failed to appear for your daily assessment of the hold. For the *third day* in a row." He heavily shook his head with overacted despair; it was typical for him, and partially why I despised him so. "I understand that you grieve, but you *cannot* be allowed to shirk your duties. Your subjects require your guidance at *all* times, my Lord."

I crossed my arms. "They can wait."

He blinked. "What?"

A smug smile crossed my lips. *Been a long time since I've surprised this old chatterbox so much that he failed to address me properly...*

"I said, 'They can wait.'"

Silas swallowed. "My Lord—please, you were always a rational man. Listen to reason. This is the earliest recorded winter on record. You have a regal obligation— nay, a *moral* obligation—to listen to their plights and give your—"

I glowered, taking a step forward. "Fine. Sit."

The elderly advisor shrunk. "My Lord?"

"*Sit*," I ordered. "In that chair. *Now*."

Silas turned over his frail shoulder to the nearby table. Kinsey merely shrugged; without a viable alternative, the old vampire pulled a chair into position, lowering himself down quietly to face me.

"Very well, my Lord. What should I do now?"

I leaned my back against the stone rail of the balcony, keeping my arms crossed. "Tell me their plights."

Silas hesitated. "My Lord—I'm not sure if—"

"Do it, Silas... or I will have you punished for *daring* to darken my personal home with your presence."

He watched me with quiet, forlorn eyes.

I spotted the moment he decided to back down.

"My Lord, I see now that this isn't a good time. Please, forgive me for my intrusion. When you are ready, if I could beseech you to come to the throne room and—"

I was off the railing in a second.

Surprising even myself, I drove a fist sideways into the stone doorway around me—spiderwebbing cracks across the large, sturdy bricks. The private suite all but trembled; everyone but Nikki jumped. "Do your job, Silas, or I will *THROW YOU FROM THIS BALCONY MYSELF!*"

He never looked so much like an old man as he did in this very moment. Silas stared up at me with pure terror, cowering in his seat like the ancient, fretting vampire that he really was.

The sight filled me with painful shame.

"Silas, I..."

I lowered my face.

I couldn't let them see my sudden humiliation, or how regret clouded my expression now. For all of his faults, the high chancellor didn't deserve this. Silas's faithful service to the royal family of Stonehold predated even my mother Lorelei's place on the throne. We had our differences, sure; but I knew in my heart that his one ambition in life was to serve the people of the realm— until the day he died.

His eyes blinked quietly. His shoulders dropped. This, I knew, was the time to apologize. The time to take this old vampire aside and build new bridges between us. He was an invaluable tool and deserving of my respect, no matter how begrudging it might come.

Instead, I darkly repeated: "*Do your job.*"

I lifted up my face and lowered my fist from the wall.

Silas stared at me with a mixture of horror and sorrow in his eyes. It wasn't just the high chancellor, either. Kinsey openly stared at me with grave disapproval. Bound by honour as she was, long before she ever became my vassal, the former royal guard couldn't hide her true feelings.

I didn't bother to turn to judge Nikki's reaction.

I felt the burn of her mesmerized, sadistic gaze against my back. *Easy to tell you've screwed up when you have **that** one's undivided attention,* I thought bitterly.

"Of course," Silas trembled. "My Lord... we, uh, have *several* orders of magnitude to discuss."

There was nothing to do now, I realized shamefully, but to commit to this path now. As I leaned my back to the railing once again, I demanded: "Go on."

Swallowing down his terror, my high chancellor spoke clearly. "The northern reaches are rapidly burning up their firewood stockades and backup heat generators. It appears that they may freeze to death over the course of winter—at least, if something isn't done."

"What are the options?"

"The options are few. You could make a decree.

Order the settlements to set aside an appropriate proportion of their excess to support the north."

"No, that won't do," I replied. "Equally unpopular and stupid. Were the winter to worsen, it would deplete their own dwindling reserves. That would unite the entire hold in suffering—not *only* those within the northern regions." I narrowed my eyes. "Give me other options."

He hesitated. "Your grandfather cared rather strongly about the balance of the nature in his reign. His restrictions and policies against unsustainable firewood practices still guide us, even now, year to year. They keep the northern forests alive and well. But if we were to—"

"Lift them."

"I... what was that, my Lord?"

"You heard me. Lift them."

"Lift the restrictions? How far?"

"Completely," I replied without hesitation.

Silas didn't even try to feign approval of that idea. "My Lord, please forgive me, but I must advise against it. If we abolish laws that protect hundreds of kilometers of woods, laws that extend back almost a millennium, it could cause *unfathomable*—"

"—Is this not the earliest winter on record?"

"I... yes, it is."

"Is it not projected to be the *coldest?*"

"That's correct, my Lord."

I waved the issue away. "Then do it. Those protections were put in place to help our people weather the harshest winters. Lift any and all restrictions against deforesting the northern regions for excess firewood. But, in doing so," I clarified firmly, "*remind* my subjects what that *means*. More wood this year means less wood the next. It takes *eons* for those trees to return. If they harvest firewood beyond what is rational, they'll be ripping life from the next generation's hearths to warm themselves. Once this winter leaves us, replanting will be necessary; I will place that responsibility firmly at the feet at those who caused it."

Silas did not reply immediately. "My Lord, you wish to remove *all* the restrictions? Surely you might want to leave *some* form of protection in place."

"*All*, Silas," I insisted. "Do **not** question me again. I will not wield a sword of law over a family that must cut down a tree to survive the winter!"

He nodded, shaken. "Of course."

I turned to Kinsey; I surveyed the turmoil in her stare. The cloud of emotion within her eyes was a mystery, even to me. My private guardian chose to finally speak up—for the first time since Silas came into my private suite.

"Do you have any need of me, Lord Elliott?"

"At the present?" I asked, surprised. "No."

"Good. Permission to rest?"

I studied her expression. *It would be too easy to deny her,*

I thought to myself. The cruelty surprised me, but it made for a rather compelling choice. *She is clearly uncomfortable. Why should she be? Make her listen. Make her watch.*

But that choice offered me no practical use.

"Granted," I replied in annoyance.

"Thank you, Lord Elliott."

We all watched as my vassal took her seat, gazing off into space. Judging by the restrained look on Silas' face, he envied her for some unapparent reason.

A devious smile crossed my lips.

"You know," I broke the silence, "I don't see why I *ever* thought this would be difficult..." I observed aloud while I drew Silas' attention back. The look on his face was one of veiled concern and alarm. "If the subjects are to turn to me for guidance, then I shall grant it..."

I noticed Nikki's wicked smirk. I ignored it.

"Silas." I crossed my arms, smirking. "What's next?"

CHAPTER 6
CLARA

The trick, I realized, was learning how to pretend.

It took me a while to get it down. Acting isn't one of those things that come naturally to me. The epiphany struck me late one night as I stared up at the biggest crack in my ceiling. It was simple, really.

I started by imagining the person I wanted to be.

First, I thought about the way she laughed. She had fire in her eyes; it radiated life at her utmost happiest. But her laugh wasn't an overbearing one; she laughed heartily but quietly, lifting her knuckles to cover her mouth.

I practiced this in the mirror.

Unfortunately, my bedroom offered nothing in the way of a decent wireless connection; it had been rubbish since I first moved here. I couldn't load up any stand-up comedy, so I instead pretended that I was listening to a good friend tell a hilarious story. I didn't have many of them anymore; I thought back to someone who used to make me laugh. The one who made me laugh the hardest was always—

For a moment, I thought of the vampire Wilhelm.

After I stopped crying, I pretended to laugh once more. With a handful of tries, I mostly got the hang of it. The girl in the mirror looked *kind* of natural.

Needs a little more work, I thought.

I moved on.

Then I realized my pretend-self still needed a smile— a natural one, too. Smiles are universal. Maybe you speak Japanese; maybe I speak English. Either way, *emotion* is the language that crosses every barrier.

The strongest tool in that language is a smile.

I sat myself down in front of the mirror, trying all kinds of smiles like samplers at a buffet. I tried out a crooked little half-smile; I pulled out a wide-eyed beam; I slipped a cheerful smirk across my lips. None of these seemed to fit properly, but I still needed to settle on one.

It was when I tried a sly smirk that I felt at home.

So, she's got some moxie, I decided.

The last one for now was the frown. That came easily —I'd had so much experience with grimaces and frowns in the past few months that *this* emotion came naturally. My radiant, smirking pretend-self tilted her head to the side, pulling down the corner of the lip and staring at me in the mirror with a death glare.

I practiced these feelings in the looking glass for a time. As I cycled through the emotions, the differences in them started to blend together—like my weeks, again.

They drifted closer together.

After half an hour or longer, and after my face began to grow numb from the exercise, the expressions seemed like they were finally coming from the same person. They were not exactly *perfect*—not yet; nevertheless, a good start.

I was proud of my progress.

As I slid back down into bed, I looked over at the black amulet on my dresser. It was my single reminder that the events in Elliott's world of vampires and magic weren't just something plucked from the depth of my imagination. That necklace came in a dream; yet, somehow, it was *real*. When I awoke from my long sleep, I found it resting under my clothes and against my collarbone.

But the amulet—and its mysterious arrival—was only part of a greater mystery. I knew it came not from Elliott's world, but *this* one. I sat up and studied it for the millionth time since returning. The amulet was a family heirloom—a ruby inset stone dangling on a black chain. It belonged to my grandmother before she passed; now, it was *mine*.

For some reason, holding it reminded me of her—but not in a nostalgic sense. I felt as if I'd seen her again, much more recently than her death... but my mind grew fuzzy, like the memory was trying to hide itself away.

I wore this amulet all the time now. I loved it. It was my one connection to the world I'd left behind—the world Elliot had taken upon himself to strip away from me.

If only you'd had more faith in yourself, Elliott, I thought. *We could have found a way. I **know** that we could have. But you went and made the decision for me, instead...*

There was nothing to gain from dwelling on this.

I shook my head and returned to my work.

When my eyes finally closed and I drifted off to sleep, dropping back into the forest chase nightmare like a rising pool, I had already memorized my pretend self. She was now just as real to me as any of those vampires—and she was better, because she was *here.*

They weren't. And they'd never be again.

She was the **only** thing that was real anymore.

IT FELT AS EASY AS FLIPPING A SWITCH IN MY HEAD.

With the lunch tray in my hands, I spotted the back of Peter's head several tables over. He was seated with a few of his other friends—I recognized them, but I didn't know them myself. Peter considerately kept the seat at his side free for me. With his back turned, I could tell that he was laughing at something with them.

"Go on," I whispered quietly to myself. "Haven't seen him today, not yet. Clara, here's your chance. Do it. Show Peter the new you."

In my mind, I visualized flowing waves of energy—colours entering my veins to invigorate me. I pictured how it came from the air, from the earth below my sneakers and the tiles, and from everyone else nearby. I imagined myself pulling a blue surge into my body like a cleansing force; likewise, I envisioned my veins themselves clogged with a reddish haze, now pushing back out, evicted and purified out from my system by the coming blue wave.

I felt my back straighten up as my posture fixed itself. I sensed my shoulders squaring as a deep, relaxing breath soaked into my lungs. *Confidence* replaced *depression* as I made myself **change** in a few deep breaths.

All the while, I pictured this newer version of myself settled into my body like a descending ghost. I felt her soak into my bones and fill my sinews, ready to guide me through the next half an hour of this lunch period.

I really wanted Peter to meet her.

After months of malaise, he deserved that.

The sly smile that slid across my face wasn't mine—

not *entirely*. It was powered by this reinvention, this mirrored version of me who hadn't suffered what I had.

I marched myself over to the table.

The others saw me first. They all glanced up at me with curious looks on their faces, as if I was a model strutting down a runway. It didn't really matter to me what their problem was—I wasn't here for them.

"Heya, Peter."

"Clara!" He glanced up at me with surprise as I took the seat next to him. Peter tilted his face curiously while I got myself settled. "How're you feeling? A bit better today, I hope?"

I flashed a smile, pulling my tray in. "*Much* better."

Peter gave me an odd look. I could tell he obviously wanted to ask me something—we were interrupted before he could find the proper words.

"You gonna introduce us, dude?"

Peter snapped out of it. "Oh. Right. Guys, this is Clara. Clara, these are some of my friends—I'm sure you've seen me talking to them around. Billy, Sam, and Packer."

Billy had his arm right around Sam as he smiled at me. Packer and Sam looked close enough in facial features to be brother and sister, and they both glanced at me with the same smile.

"You two. Siblings?"

"Twins," Packer nodded.

Sam added: "Fraternal."

I smirked slyly. "Knew it. I could tell you were related. You've got the same look in your eyes."

"Yeah?" Sam asked. "What do you mean?"

"It's, uh, a bit hard to put into words," I shrugged. "I used to know a pair of twins when I was a kid—these two beautiful girls. Identical. You couldn't tell them apart at all that easily, but they both had that same kind of connected thing in their eyes. We called it a 'twinly twinkle'."

"What. We have that?" Packer turned, looking into his sister's eyes.

"I say that you do," I nodded.

Billy looked amused; he gazed around the table. "You know, now that you mention it, that kinda sounds right. I just couldn't put my finger on it before."

Peter was still looking at me funnily.

"What's the matter?" I met his gaze slyly.

"You're different today."

"Yeah, well..." I examined the floppy slice of pizza on my lunch tray. It didn't exactly inspire anticipation. "Maybe I decided to stop moping around," I shrugged.

"No, it's not that. You seem... I can't tell."

"Oh, let the poor girl eat," Billy chuckled.

"Yeah, Peter," I ribbed him lightly. "You know what kind of gruel my stepdad makes me eat back at home. Let me enjoy this cooking masterpiece in peace, yeah?"

"*Masterpiece?*" Packer chuckled.

I chewed a rubbery chunk of stale, cafeteria pizza.

"You know, Evanshire Academy's lunches have slowly become the culinary highlight of my daily life," I replied. The absurdity of it almost made me laugh. I swallowed the sad little bite of pizza, flashing a defeated smile in Peter's direction. "How far does your life have to fall to make *that* a fact? How disappointing is *that?*"

"Clara…" He started, confused.

"Who *is* this chick?" Billy laughed.

Sam watched me carefully, her eye squinting.

"You're Clara *Blackwell*, right?"

I shot her a raised eyebrow. "Guilty as charged."

"Yeah!" She nodded repeatedly, tapping a finger in the air to the timing of her nods. "You're Clara! You're that girl who went missing for, like, a month!" The others looked at me with fresh eyes.

Deep inside, I felt a part of me scream.

But that part wasn't the part I put in control now; this newer, better version of myself could laugh off anything, even if it was simply being known for the tragedy that was steadily ruining my life.

Peter cleared his throat. "Clara, I, uh…"

"You're right," I smirked as I shoved that part of me deep down. "You got me, Sam. I'm that girl who showed up half-drowned on the edge of a lake."

"Wow," Packer noted. "You're taking *that* well."

I chuckled—eager to keep my momentum still going. "The way that I look at it, I've got two options, right? I can either let what happened out there dictate my life..." I tore off another bite of pizza with my teeth and swallowed it. "Or I can move past it and get on with things."

Sam looked teary-eyed. "That's... admirable."

"Yeah, pretty amazing," Billy replied, turning to Peter. "Dude. Why haven't you introduced us to her until *today?* She's freaking great!"

Peter turned knowingly, answering half of that.

"Yeah, she is."

I briefly arched an eyebrow at him.

"Can't keep me to yourself *all* the time, right?"

All his friends smiled at us. I couldn't help but notice Sam and Packer specifically grinning in unison. Peter held up his hands in defeat.

"Alright, alright! I know when to fold 'em..."

The table lifted all lifted their drinks in cheers.

It felt good to push everything down. The crippling depression threatening to drag me into the deepest pits of my inner darkness felt a lot lighter now. Of course, I knew that it wasn't, not really. This was an illusion; this version of myself wasn't *actually* me. She was nothing more than a whisper of smoke in the dark, a reflection through a haze.

But, with time, maybe this *could* be the real me after all. I just had to keep up this façade until my original self was little more than ashes. Maybe it wasn't the healthy choice, but this was all that I had now. I needed it to get me past this one, single day. With practice, and a little dedication, I imagined it could get me past *every* day.

Peter looked at me, and I smiled at him.

I could see the concern in his eyes.

My smile nearly faltered.

CHAPTER 7

NIKKI

Chrysm always looked hellish to me.

I lay on my back against the hard, frigid floor in the chrysm hub, surrounded by a semi-circle of five teleportation nodes. Distantly, I slid my foot back and forth as I stared up at the glass pipes. As my boot came in proximity, the red glow of the node flickered to life; when I dragged my foot away, the node dissolved its glimmer and drifted back to dormancy.

Bare crimson ore kind of always struck me as if it were filled with blood. Processed chrysm—the really good stuff, and the primary energy source to the entire world—was even more nightmarish at a glance.

These nodes all grew a column of crimson light as they activated, as if they would take you somewhere awful. But they never did. They took you where you wanted to go.

Well, okay. They took us *Cravens* wherever we wanted.

It was telling that all the tubes and channels that ran it beneath the castle were buried by design. The liquid form, pumping through its pipes, reminded me of flowing blood through the fleshy wires along the vampiric body. The only times we saw natural chrysm was in the light fixtures, before the filters changed the reddish glow into something more pleasing to the eyes. You only got a glimpse at its true color down here, of course—but so few members of the castle ever got to see the beating heart of the island.

After all—who wants to live somewhere with every room bathed in a nice, hellish glow?

Who besides *me*, I guess.

I remember fearing the chrysm nodes when I was still a child. The teleportation system set up across the castle by my mother, the vampire lord, was designed to let the royal family—and *only* the royal family—move around instantly within the sprawling stronghold.

To my young, naive mind, it was unnatural, unsettling. The burning radiance haunted my nightmares, threatening to drag me far beneath the ground, down to this atrium of processed chrysm ore—filled with clanging machines and bright, towering screens.

Even as an adult, it made me uneasy.

But then came the accident.

My magical affinity had always been less of a blessing, more of a curse. I needed to keep my emotions forever in check, because I lost control of the powerful forces in my blood when I let my temper flare.

The time that I *really* lost it, I lost *everything*.

My place on the island.

My older sister.

My *sanity*.

Keeping my thoughts straight was a daily struggle. My head was constantly filled with devilish impulses to twist and destroy, and I craved the taste of fresh blood— not just saved and preserved, but the kind I *earned*. The sweetest blood, the most *satisfying* blood, was that from the darkest wilds beyond our settlements... where I'd have to tackle a predator to the ground and best it in a fight to the death.

I craved the hunt.

I craved the *kill*.

And after a hundred years on the Stonehold mainland, I had become *very* good at hunting the vicious wildlife that could destroy us all if we allowed it to run rampant. Still, our hold was rather tame in that department; in the others, I'd heard stories of wild beasts so malicious and heinous that they'd make your *toes* curl...

But that prospect only excited me.

Well after the accident splintered my mind, I no longer knew fear the way I once had. The red glow of the chrysm was equally hellish as before, but where it made me fear for my life in the past? Now, it comforted me.

The crimson aura felt like home. It felt kindred.

It occurred to me that I'd probably been on the floor for hours with these nodes, down within the primary atrium. Satisfied, I pulled myself to my feet and stepped onto the round platform, watching it come to life beneath me...

৩৯৯

As the red glow of the chrysm node evaporated, I found myself surrounded by ancient bookcases.

I stepped down the stairs from the node and let the familiar smell of old books drown my senses. I welcomed the change. The scent of ancient tomes always brought me back to earlier days as a young vampire, when I spent so much of my time exploring all the very darkest nooks and crannies of the castle I called home.

This library had so *many* of them. I'd quickly grown a healthy love for its ancient maze of bookcases—walls filled with hardcover tomes that, more frequent than not, hadn't been moved in centuries.

To a small extent, it fascinated me that the culmination of our history, our knowledge, and all of our fiction was centralized to this massive study, one buried in the darkest depths of the island. Even our dungeons were closer to the sun than this underground network of chambers.

Of course, there was a practical reason for that.

If Stonehold Castle were to ever be seriously attacked, we wanted our knowledge protected. There was no place deeper in the entire stronghold than this place. It was said that the destruction of a hold ended with the annihilation of its castle library. Even severing off a bloodline with war and gleaming metal didn't guarantee the region's end... or so they said. I wasn't a vampire lord. I didn't really know these things for sure.

Burn it down, my madness told me.

For a fleeting moment, I seriously considered it.

No, I ultimately decided. *I like the books.*

I made my way into the heart of the library, seeking the master of the ancient texts. The Sage of Stonehold was recognized as the wisest vampire in the entire hold, and I wondered how criminally underused he was down here while Elliott sulked atop his tower.

*Well, that's not fair. I know what he's **really** up to...*

It wasn't hard to find Sebastian. I'd been down here a handful of times in the months since we sent Clara back to her own world, mostly for...

I guess I didn't know why.

Stepping into his flowing study, I sensed in an instant that something was wrong. The elderly Sage of Stonehold sat motionlessly behind his desk, dressed in robes that just *screamed* 'wise old man.' Sebastian's bushy gray beard was draped down his front—and I noticed then that his kind, blue eyes gazed dully ahead without seeing.

I was disappointed.

"You're not dead, are you?"

Sebastian didn't move.

With a heavy sigh, I pulled over a chair and kicked up my boots atop the edge of his desk. He had been in the middle of eating—I reached over and took an apple, biting into it with a satisfying crunch.

"It wasn't your fault, you know," I told him.

He didn't respond.

"It wasn't mine, either."

Nothing.

"If we're gonna get technical here, I don't know *who* deserves the blame," I shrugged. The apple was too crisp to ignore, so I crunched into it again. "Sabine, for trying to steal her? Or was it my brother, for giving the order to cast her away? Maybe both. Maybe nobody."

Sebastian's motionless body sat in dead silence.

"All I know is that everything's gone to hell. The world hangs at the brink of a disaster that never got around to actually happening. We all knew it at the time, didn't we?" Swallowing another chunk, I gazed at him as if he could offer an answer now. "We could see that flinging Clara away was a mistake. But fancy trying to convince the great 'Lord Craven' of that when he's buried up to his waist in *good intentions,* with his mind all made up..."

Sebastian snapped to alertness, blinking at me.

"Oh good," I chuckled. "Guess you're alive after all."

"Lady Craven?" He asked. "How long have I...?"

"I forget that you used to be a royal guard," I thought aloud as I took another hard bite into the apple. *I'm swiftly running out of apple...* "Your little zoning-out trick. They all have that. The tinkering they do with your head must've all been worked out even before *your* time..."

"The last thing that I remember is when you were here, when I last..." He glanced up at me sullenly. "My Lady, do you know how long was I gone?"

I answered obliquely. "A minute? A day? A century?"

Sebastian's expression saddened. He glanced away in a sour mood. I knew exactly what was going on his ancient, battered mind—and even the compulsively dark whispers in my head quieted down out of respect.

"You know, it's dangerous to slip into a trance like that from a place of grief," I reminded the sage, playing with a little callousness on my tongue. It felt good to tell him off so decisively, even it was true. "Strong feelings of sadness are a powerful enhancer for tricks like that. You'll fade away far too deeply to *ever* come back..."

"I'm aware, Lady Craven," he sighed.

"I know you're aware. Doesn't mean you don't need a

reminder on occasion." Hastily, I pulled my boots back off the table edge, leaning forward. "Tell me how it feels."

"Hmm?" He looked up at me.

I felt an evil glint in my gaze. "To sleep like that."

Sebastian eyed me cautiously, studying my eyes. "You know, my Lady, I never grasped why you of all have such a reputation for your sadism. These past few months that you've visited me, I've known all along that you've been on your very best behaviour—but with a little gleam like that, in your eyes right now..."

"Yes?" I asked, tilting my head.

Sighing, he shook his head at me. "I can finally see why the others tread so lightly around you."

My eyes narrowed, but my smile widened.

A part of me deep down seemed saddened to hear that. But that was the old me—from before the magical accident that forced me into exile. *I would have thought* **everybody** *knew the stories of what happened that day, especially the sage—and of what happened* **afterwards**...

"You didn't answer my question," I noticed.

Sebastian wearily smiled. "It's like sleeping."

"Oh?" I tilted my head again. "Tell me more."

"A deep and powerful sleep. Comforting, even." The sage smiled wearily to himself. "Enticing..."

I finished off the apple, tossing it into a bin. "You have gotta snap out of it, old man.'

He glanced glumly at me. "What do you mean?"

"You ready for a little brutal honesty?" I crossed my leg over the other and leaned back into my chair. "Like I said during your, uh, little nap there—it was not your fault, Sebastian. Wasn't mine either. Neither of us could have done anything to change Elliott's mind."

"I feel as if I've done nothing but hurt that girl."

"Nonsense," I snarled. "Under direct orders, you found the spell that protected her from all the bloody vampires in the castle. No harm in that."

"It cast her into a coma."

I shrugged. "She got *better*."

"She was asleep for *days*."

"Like I said. She got better."

"I also found the spell that sent her away..."

"You forget," I leaned closer. "Who *cast* that spell?"

He looked away. "You did, Nikki."

It wasn't like him to use our given names without the proper titles—and that's when I smirked, knowing I had his attention. "How do you think that makes *me* feel?"

Sebastian didn't offer a response.

"And let's not forget that our *darling* mother decided to pack her bags and vanish off without a trace the following day." I threw my hands up in complete disgust. "That one moment in time destroyed our lives."

"What do you mean?"

I laughed darkly. "Do I have to spell it out for you? On top of all else we face now, have you gone feeble in your sadness? I can't have you going decrepit on me, too."

Sebastian took a deep breath, and I sighed.

"Fine then," I muttered sadly. "Clara's gone forever. Elliott is up there with his private little statue, brooding in the tower. You're stuck way down here but, let's be honest, you're *always* down here; Mum's disappeared; those three royal guards Clara liked so much have been separated and banished overseas, and then there was that sorceress..."

"The one who turned on us?"

"Yes. The one who's dead now."

"Are you counting her?"

I deliberated. "Guess not. Screw her."

Sebastian nodded calmly. "I agree that this was a grave mistake. The human girl's disappearance has had an effect over the castle we couldn't possibly have anticipated."

"No... but we've gotten lucky so far."

"Right," he noted. "The vampire lords..."

I could feel a murderous impulse rise in the back of my mind. HE'S OLD AND WEAK. YOU'RE ALONE WITH HIM...

"No," I twisted my head. "Stop it."

"Stop what?"

I blinked at the sage. "Nothing."

He sighed. "Your impulses?"

"...*Maybe.*"

"What are they telling you to do?"

It was better to ignore that question. Grinning a sly, evil little smile, I reached over to take another apple from the sage's desk. "Do you know why I love these so much?"

"I would have thought it was the taste."

I chuckled. "I like the crunch."

"Is that so?"

"It reminds me of the snapping of bones."

Sebastian shook his head, his eyes still watching mine. "Biting an apple and breaking a bone sound *nothing* alike, Lady Craven. You know this as well as any among us."

My eye squinted as I smirked at him, taking a fresh bite of the crisp fruit in my hand. "Let a girl pretend."

The sage shook his head sorrowfully. "I have known you since you were a young child. Long before your first equinox... always such a loving creature. It pains me to see how you've devolved into this. How did you ever become this way?"

I laughed evilly. "Killing my sister helped."

Sebastian conceded that point. After a private moment of thought, he asked: "Why do you come down here?"

Feeling a strong sense of loss, I turned away from the Sage of Stonehold. "Clara was the only one to really accept me as what I am, flaws and all... I think it helped me."

Sebastian stroked his beard. "Explains a few things. Maybe *that's* why you haven't been so erratic lately."

"You and I are the ones that sent my friend away. That means you're the only one who understands."

Sebastian reached a reassuring hand out.

"That's not a good idea," I told him.

"Try me."

Hesitantly, I looked down at his open palm. Elderly and weak, it flexed reassuringly. With a soft sigh, I put my hand in his and tried to fight back the impulses.

They didn't take very long to rise in my head.

I spoke reluctantly. "I'm going to hurt you."

"No, you're not."

The whispers came. CRUSH IT.

"No," I shook my head.

FEEL IT SHATTER IN YOUR GRIP.

"Stop it," I bit down on my lip.

All the while, Sage Sebastian quietly watched my eyes. I hated how he just looked at me. *You stupid old man —why aren't you taking this seriously?* That time, I couldn't tell if the thought was really mine or not. The madness had such a way of distorting my mind beyond recognition...

JUST CLOSE YOUR HAND. AS HARD AS YOU CAN...

"Let go," I told him. "Now, before—"

My veins filled with malice when I grinned mercilessly, clenching my grip as hard as I could. I was suddenly eager to utterly break apart every bone in his hand...

"Huh?" I growled, looking at it in my own.

Sebastian merely watched me.

I snarled then, squeezing at maximum strength; every ounce of rage poured into my supernatural grip.

"Why won't your bones snap?" I shouted with a mix of anger and anguish.

"You forget, my dear Lady Craven," he replied calmly. "I have the body of an old and frail vampire, but I'm eight hundred ninety-seven years old. Despite appearances, I'm not a weakling. I am as strong as *ever*."

"But I have the blood of a vampire lord," I protested.

"Indeed," he noted calmly, nodding to himself. "And I am the Sage of Stonehold. Would you not believe, with all the reading material at my disposal, that I have not picked up a *few* tricks?"

I released my grip from him. "I can't hurt you?"

"Not *easily*," he conceded.

"Then you *might* be the only vampire in the castle who I can't overwhelm in strength alone... well, maybe besides our sulking lord in Craven Keep."

"How does that make you feel?" He asked.

"Part of me wants to kill you for it."

Sebastian chuckled, arching up an eyebrow. "That's so, is it? What about the other parts?"

"Relieved," I sighed wearily. "I have been all by myself for so long out there; it's been hard to be around any of the others. I've steered myself clear of the staff, lest I begin to pick them off, one by one..."

"So, you wander down to see me instead?"

"Not for you. I'm here all the time, reading the books. I've come to this place almost every day since I returned to the castle. You can't expect to hoard this kind of power all to yourself, you greedy old coot. Besides, maybe if I keep reading, I'll figure out your little parlour tricks..."

"And, with luck, I will keep on surprising you," the old man replied with a smile.

I chuckled, leaning closer to him again. "I guess that I *do* come to see you a lot. You're probably the only vampire who truly understands what I've gone through."

Sebastian nodded. "We are united by grief."

"United by grief. How poetic. I could agree with that. Maybe I won't kill you today."

"That would be much appreciated," he replied.

For ages after those words, we sat together in silence, deep down within the castle library—and in our silence, we mourned the mistake that we made together.

CHAPTER 8
CLARA

Erily, the dark dream forest stood calmly silent.

I wasn't even running—I stood in place.

It was so startling to realize this that I very nearly slipped in place and fell to the mulched forest floor. Instead, I just managed to barely keep my footing stable. With all my suspicions running at an all-time high, I took a tentative step forward, then another.

I peered through the trees all around me.

Nothing.

"What on Earth..."

There was no denying it. This was the forest from my nightmares—but it still lacked one historic piece, the most defining part of the puzzle I'd yet to have solved.

The murderous force had gone missing.

Without it here, I had time to glance around at my

surroundings. I remembered that I always started off at this exact spot in the dream; there, a mossy, outcropping boulder stuck out at me like a landmark.

"Then that means..."

I turned.

This way was the way I always ran, trying to escape the unseen creature that stalked me. But when I realized that I was in the dream, I was already running this direction.

I'd never seen any of the rest of the forest.

Eager to take swift advantage of this, I hooked a right and began walking that way instead. It didn't seem like the new direction changed very much.

The further I walked, and the longer I spent here, the more that I felt the presence of something dwelling on my mind—like a small pebble in my sneaker. To some small degree, I was lucidly aware that I had overlooked some major detail. I couldn't tell what it was; it bothered me to be aware of it without seeing. The harder that I tried, the further away my realization seemed to be.

It was when I finally gave up that I recalled a lost spark of memory. *Lying in my bed, the amulet around my throat. Willing myself to sleep, willing myself to be in control...*

I gasped with dawning comprehension.

I did it, I grinned ecstatically. *I took back control*—even if it only ***partially*** worked, naturally. Sure, I might have held back the predatory malevolence that haunted my waking nightmares, but I still found myself trapped in the same recurring dream.

Is it because I willed this through the amulet...?

I grasped at my collarbone. There, the amulet hung at my neck. I had never noticed it within my nightmare, and I wasn't quite sure what do with that information.

Well, I thought to myself triumphantly. *I guess that I'd better make the most of this...*

I STUDIED THE FOREST AS I WALKED.

The blind terror that filled me every night had always stopped me from paying attention to the woods. I didn't grasp until then just how clearly I could see the trees. This wasn't some hazy, indistinct nightmare like all the others; had the dream always been this sharp and *real?*

It was like walking through a high-definition hallucination. It seemed more lifelike than it should, this prison of my mind. The trembling trees stood sharply against the dark shadows, their bark powerfully gnarled and their roots gnarled with striking detail. Even all the underbrush surrounding me seemed carefully designed. Darkness was on all sides, but I realized just how clearly I could see.

I'd *always* seen clearly here—dodging roots that should have tripped me far more often than they did, or pulling through weeds and bushes that I never lost myself in.

"I wonder why that is," I spoke to myself.

Even my voice seemed unnaturally clear.

"Am I honestly asleep?"

I thought back to a little trick I'd heard from a woman I could barely remember, locked away from my usual grasp of memory. The woman was older and very powerful; if I recalled correctly, she talked to me about dreams as we walked through a beautiful garden...

A memory of Elliott Craven flashed in my head.

Was she someone like him?

I couldn't remember a face or a name; yet, I could still remember the words, when I had talked of attempting to pinch myself awake in my dreams...

"Pinching never works. Learn how your palm feels as you run your finger down it. It's far subtler. Mimic that in your dreams, and see how the sensation feels."

I already knew what I'd feel as I did it.

Nothing. So it was true. I was really asleep.

Parts of the forest dream came back to me then, and I decided to go visit the ocean. I picked the right direction and passed through the woods, taking my time to move around thorns and branches and snares that never actually hurt me, but that always made me fear this place when my adrenaline was pumping.

Without running, it took a lot longer than usual. At my leisure, I broke through the tree-line to see the cliff. Far in the distance rested a familiar island.

"Dream-Elliott *did* always demand that I make my way to that island," I recalled. "I wonder what's really there."

Despite my new awareness, I knew I wasn't capable of changing anything about this place. That clearly included the rolling waves and the sharp rocks down below. From my vantage point, I could still barely see the island.

Maybe it was the distance, but it didn't really strike me as very significant. It just seemed like a dark, remote point of interest against an otherwise vast and endless sea, and brightly lit beneath the full moon.

The mystery remained locked to me.

I walked back along the edge of the trees. After a while, it was obvious that there was nothing to be gained and no more to be seen, so I stepped back into the forest proper. In my surprise, I faintly recognized a bush here, and a thicket there—I pulled back and left the tree-line again.

The jutting of the rocks confirmed my suspicions. I'd re-entered where I'd first stepped onto the cliff.

"What do I make of that?" I asked no one.

There's nothing else along the cliff, I realized. *The cliff isn't important. Otherwise, I'd be able to explore it, or I'd probably find* **something** *interesting along the edge...*

So, I went back the way I came, wanting to try a new direction. With the dream frozen in time, the opportunities were rife to see this place as it truly was. After some time, I came back to the original clearing in which I always found myself running for my life. As I gazed around the trail, it occurred to me how strange it was to always be in this spot, always fleeing from the very start of the dream.

I sat down on a nearby stump and wondered.

"Dreams..." I gazed up at the full moon—it was still hanging in view, at least from the clearing. "They never really start from the *beginning*, do they?"

No answer came for me.

I looked around at the woods as they surrounded me. Nothing seemed out of the ordinary, but I felt the oddest sensation that I was still being watched, somehow.

But there's nothing here.

Nothing **alive**, *at any rate...*

"If I had to guess..." I addressed myself, "I'd wonder if there was actually something more to this dream I couldn't ever remember. If this is always the same exact nightmare, I guess that means there's something here to trigger all the chaos—something that I can never retain before I realize that I'm running away."

The forest, again, offered me no reply. It didn't need to. I felt I was finally beginning to *understand,* just *maybe...*

I bounced up from the stump and dusted myself off; I marched myself in the opposite direction that I always ran. *There's nothing else to find here, unless there's a little something **this** way...*

It wasn't long off a walk before I learned that there was something wrong. It seemed that every couple of strides, the forest faded away—but it was truly the strangest thing. It wasn't that the darkness was growing, or that the forest was disappearing, necessarily... it was like something else *overcame* the forest. The surrounding trees grew fewer and further between. There was no canopy above anymore, just the bright full moon without a cloud in the night sky. The underbrush thinned out to nearly nothing, leaving the forest floor next to empty. But the moon steadily dimmed, too. The way forward was ever fuzzier, and I felt a sense of ominous dread overcoming me.

I turned back.

Relief came settling in as I started taking larger strides, rapidly restoring the forest back around me. It didn't come all at once, nor did it magically just appear at my feet as I headed back that way. Instead, the trees began at a logical point, growing denser until the dream forest surrounded me once again.

"Well that's weird." I looked over my shoulder.

The dread rose again when I marched myself back in that direction. I had to know what it was hiding out there, no matter how my chest tightened.

This time, I pushed forward.

The forest once again grew sparser until it was gone. The floor of the woods beneath my feet faded away to a featureless black, and soon there was nothing left but the moon above—a moon that only grew dimmer and darker with every step.

The mounting dread heightened until I could almost hear it—a buzzing in my ears that rose in pitch until...

"Wait," I stopped.

The moon was almost totally gone now.

But I *could* hear it.

For a moment of horrible, eye-widening realization, I was overcome with a sudden awareness of *something*. For the briefest second, I felt I instantly comprehended what it was that was in my nightmare with me. It struck my heart with the blackest, darkest terror I'd ever felt in my life.

The moment passed, and I ran back.

I didn't stop until I was in the clearing.

For the longest couple of seconds of my life, I stood utterly *terrified* I would feel that malevolent force rising in the dark, rushing back towards me to bring down its utter destruction like always before. Unspeakable relief slowly filled my lungs when I gathered that it wasn't happening. The dream really *was* still locked. I was safe.

And then, I realized what I needed to do.

MY EYES DARTED AWAKE BESIDE THE PILLOW.

I leapt straight out of bed, eager to remember every last detail of what I'd just experienced. Frantic and fearful, my half-asleep body dove across the room and dug through my drawers until I had my hands on the forgotten diary.

And then I began to write.

Out of the desperate scribbling from my pen, scrawling words slowly took over the page. Determined to save as much of the dream as I could, I let the hurried madness overtake my hand—until my wrist cramped up.

I could remember no more.

I reread what I had written. Already, it was all fading away from my head. But the words were here. If I really wanted to see Elliott Craven in my dreams again...

I finally knew what had to be done.

Affectionately, I brushed my fingertips along the edge of the book. A small layer of dust wiped off as I touched the tough cover, wrapped in felt and still stiff from lack of use. "I've been using you all wrong, haven't I? Here I was, thinking you were meant to be a day journal all along... but you're a *dream diary*, aren't you?"

The diary didn't respond—but the amulet did.

For a split second, it seemed to glow in reply...

CHAPTER 9
ELLIOTT

I sat up in bed after yet another restless slumber.

My haggard eyes caught the timepiece sitting at my bedside, then the window. It was the middle of the day, but there was no way to tell with the blackened sky. The stars twinkled far above; there was no daylight left to brighten the air.

It has finally come.

Grunting, I rose from my bedding. My movements felt sluggish, and my limbs weary; I'd spent most of the night drinking myself into a stupor. I scratched my bare chest as I walked into the bathroom and saw myself in the mirror.

I didn't recognize the face that stared back.

Exhausted, bloodshot eyes scowled back at me. In their fatigue, I noticed the shattered carcass of a broken man's spirit. Its clothes were ruffled and stained with

blood; the pale skin showed hints of the veins promi-
nently threaded under its throat and at its wrists.

I reached a trembling hand for it—the creature
staring back did the same, distrustfully watching my
fingertips. The thing in my reflection looked like it was
pushed to the brink and stood at death's door. Hideous
and ill, it glared into my eyes with bitter disappointment.

"Who are you to judge me?" I demanded.

A fang protruded. Its eyes darkened furiously. There
would be no answer from this beast that confronted me;
but that would simply not do. I wondered if I could take
it, if it chose to lunge for me. It looked far too sick to put
up a fight—but I felt so very tired.

"I asked you a question," I ordered, raising my voice
defiantly. "I said, 'Who are *you* to judge me?'"

The face broke into a vicious scream; it terrified the
living daylights out of me. I stumbled back from the
glass, tripping and falling against the back wall in horror.

It was gone as soon as it appeared.

"Damn my imagination," I growled, stumbling.

I pulled myself up. Hesitant to see the mirror again, I
avoided my reflection. I kept my eyes closed, washing my
face with hot water in the basin. When they finally
opened again, the face that glared at me this time looked
a lot more agreeable.

"A smidge better," I growled.

Scowling, I dropped my sleeping clothes to the floor

and stepped into the blisteringly hot shower. Twisting the various selection of knobs, handles, and levers to my distinct liking, I closed my eyes and let the water run through my hair and down my body—meanwhile, the apertures on the ceiling began randomly adjusting, and the temperature slid through various levels of heat.

"*Ahhh*," I grinned to myself with closed eyes, running my fingers through thick hair. *This is not that complicated of a device,* I thought nonchalantly. *I wonder how Clara could **possibly** have had trouble figuring out—*

My eyes flew open and I snarled.

It was only when I felt the slight pain in my hand that I realized I'd punched my fist into the wall. Judging by the cracking tile, I must have done it several times— enough to overwhelm my advanced strength and *pain* tolerance.

"She will never come back," I snapped to nobody else. "You sent her away, you fool. She's gone forever."

There was no reply. *Of course there's no reply. You've sent them all away, haven't you? You got rid of the human, and you divided her guardians and sent them away as well...*

Annoyed, I scrubbed my skin clean, washing the traces of exhaustion away. My soaking fingers slipped back into my hair as I vigorously washed, clearing my mind of all of these troublesome things. After I finally stepped out of the shower chamber, I dried myself off and wrapped the towel tight around my waist.

Twenty minutes later, I finished threading my boots and stepped into the dining area of my royal suite. As I'd come to expect, my vassal sat at the table, staring off into space near the balcony.

"Awaken," I ordered.

Kinsey blinked. "How may I serve, my Lord—?"

The vampire paused when she saw me.

"What's the matter?" I asked coolly.

"Nothing," she shook her head. "It's just…"

I crossed my arms and awaited a response.

"It's been a long time since I've seen you taking care of yourself again, Lord Elliott," Kinsey finished. "What's the occasion?"

"The occasion?" I chuckled darkly. "I've grown weary of these walls. I feel that a change of scenery might do me some good."

"Oh? Where would you like to go?"

"My throne room, to start."

She rose from her chair, surprised. "Of course."

"But, if you *must* know…" I let my glance drift over to the balcony doors. They stood wide open, just how I'd left them last night when I wondered how many times I might have to drop from that railing to actually break a bone, let alone my own neck. "The light has left. The winter is now permanent darkness. If I remain in this tower *one more day*, I'll go absolutely bloody mad."

"I was wondering how long it might take."

"Oh?" I cast her a vicious glance.

She almost shrugged. "It's easier for me. Far as I'm concerned, it's only been hours. Maybe a day?"

"It's been four months," I grimaced.

"Permission to speak?"

An eye twitched. *What now?* "Granted."

"Let's not make it *five,* Lord Elliott," she smirked.

I almost smiled back. Instead, I turned and clicked my fingers. "Come along, my vassal. Perpetual night has risen, and I am called to action. Let us see how much the fools in the castle miss me."

Kinsey fell into step beside me as we made our way towards my personal chrysm node.

"It's good to see you back, Lord Elliott."

"Perhaps you'll change your mind."

"I have faith in you," she replied. "I'm sure I won't."

She *did* change her mind...

But it took a while.

FOR ALL PURPOSES OF PRESENTATION, THERE STOOD A wall between the throne and the receiving chrysm node.

Whenever I left or returned to the hall, my passing was disguised—I could arrive on the node, turn a corner, and be seated in the throne in mere seconds. It made for a sort of startling effect when unexpected.

Naturally, this is precisely what I did.

"Five," I lazily counted from a slouch. "Six... *seven...*"

Every guard in the room suddenly stood at attention. The captain rushed over to my throne, dropping to a knee. "My Lord! Forgive me—we weren't expecting you back in the throne room so soon!"

"When *were* you expecting me?"

She chuckled. "Would you like me to lie?"

My eyes snapped to a glare.

"Oh... I'm sorry, I... don't know why I thought—"

"No, go on," I smirked defiantly. "Tell me."

"My Lord?"

"Tell me when you were expecting me."

"Soon," she replied hastily. "Very soon."

"The next time that you *lie* to me," I tilted my head and raised an eyebrow, "I will order my vassal here to run her spear through your armor. Don't worry. You'll survive. You'll even make a full recovery. But perhaps you'll learn a lesson or two about lying to your liege."

It did not escape my notice how Kinsey turned to look at the back of my head.

The captain swallowed.

"Tell me," I repeated.

"Forgive me, my Lord..." I saw how she trembled. "I don't wish to make you repeat yourself, but I... seem to have forgotten the question."

I smiled. It felt good to make her fear me.

"*When* where you expecting me?" I asked again.

She steeled herself. "Maybe never."

With a smile plastered on my face, I felt it start deep down at the bottom of my chest. It worked its way up my lungs as I snorted—as my shoulders began to bounce, I tried in vain to hold it back. But then I felt it explode out my mouth. My head rolled back as heaving laughter overcame me. Covering my forehead with a hand, I threaded my fingers into my hair as the uncontrollable laughter roared across the throne room.

When I finally regained my composure, I slid back into my regal slouch on the throne. A few stray chuckles stuck to my parted lips; I slid my tongue along a fang.

I turned to Kinsey, who stood dutifully at my side.

"How long has it been since I've laughed?"

She turned away to think. "A while."

"Days? Weeks?"

"Upwards of half a year, I'd imagine."

"Right..." I turned back to the guard captain. "Suffice to say, I believe I needed that laugh. I don't see much point in punishing you for your complete insolence."

The captain paled—hard for a vampire to do, that. "Thank you, my Lord. I promise that will be the last time I make you laugh for a long while."

I smirked. "You're a fast learner, aren't you?"

"Yes, my Lord. I... like to think so."

I'd grown bored of this already.

"What is your name?"

She blinked. "My Lord, my name is—"

"Nevermind," I waved my wrist. "Divide your guards as you see fit. Send them all across the castle. Within the next hour, I want every royal guard within these walls to understand that I have returned to my rightful place."

"O-of course, my Lord."

She called over the guards lining the walls.

Meanwhile, I turned to Kinsey, sensing her discomfort. "What is it?" Darkly, I added: "I don't need a *human* in my presence to feel that you disapprove."

"Is it wise to send them all away?"

"The guards?" I shrugged. "Well, here's one of the most fortified chambers in the entire castle. The only thing that can get into this room against my wishes is one of the other vampire lords, and if one of *them* decides to pay me a visit, well..." I chuckled in amused defeat. "It'd take half the guards on the island to keep one of them at bay. Any less than that would be a massacre."

"It is not often that this room is so undefended."

*This one's adorable. Why didn't I just make her a vassal **ages** ago?* "There has been little to defend for a very long time," I reminded her. "Perhaps a little 'risking fate' is in order."

Kinsey's lips thinned.

She didn't dare to question any further.

"You have more to say," I obliquely noted. "Go on."

She sighed. "'*Risking fate,*' Lord Elliott? Would you not say that staying confined to your tower this long did not already qualify as '*risking fate?*' You speak of the other vampire lords with great respect of their power—what if they had chosen to come while you were away?"

"You act as if you did not see it with your eyes. I was never far. Silas gave me daily updates on the other holds—with the difficulties facing the world, my enemies will be kept busier still for the foreseeable future. We will settle our grievances at another time."

"You sound like you're counting on that."

"I am."

"But, is that... *wise?*"

"It is," I insisted. "I have had plenty of time to grieve. The light has completely left our land and we are facing a winter beyond anything on record. I am finished giving decrees from my bedroom. The day has come to be more... *proactive* with my rule."

"I hope it's not too late."

For a moment, I faintly considered letting her in on my ulterior motives, and what I'd *really* been doing atop that tower—while she spent all her days disappearing into the statuesque sleep of the royal guards. Then again, she had questioned me—and I did not see fit to reward such lack of faith with answers.

"You have now had your chance to speak your mind," I warned Kinsey. "Do not make a habit of faltering in your commitments to serving me, or I will demote you from your position—and the punishments for a failed vassal are a tad more *severe* than you'd find comfortable."

Her face restrained into a dutiful, placid nod.

"Of course, my Lord."

A flicker of remorse flew across my heart. A part of me, deep down, regretted treating her like this. *She is the only one who speaks her mind anymore. Maybe I shouldn't stomp that out—second opinions are valuable, and Kinsey has proven her worth beyond question.*

Besides, what would Clara think—?

The door snapped shut on my heart.

Forget it, I shook my head.

I vowed then: every time I thought of my lost lover, I would tighten the seal on my heart another click of the lock. It was the only way to survive this fracture inside me—and the only way to keep Stonehold safe.

It felt natural to agree with that sentiment.

That's right. It's the only way.

CHAPTER 10
CLARA

Decmber came—the end of a long year that had changed my world forever, only for it to drop me depressingly back into the utterly mundane by comparison. I had now been home for six months.

During the nights, I practiced my dream control.

I learned a few things here.

It was clear that the black amulet itself was the key. During the evenings when I slept without it, I endured my nightmares and all their brutality *without* fail.

Furthermore, it wasn't as easy as just wearing the thing around my neck. I had to *will* my amulet to work, and that in itself was tiring. Didn't always work every night, either. I had a few theories for that. Perhaps the amulet outright refused, as if it had a mind of its own...

or maybe it was my fault that I couldn't find enough of the energy to hold back the malevolent force.

Still, for the first time in a long time, I slept soundly. Even my failures could not break the hope that steadily rose inside me. I hadn't cracked the code to bring Elliott's shadow back into my dreams, but I was close.

I was gaining power over my *nights*.

As for the ***days***...

I grew steadily more comfortable with the imaginary self that I'd invented. My mind had adapted to the change quickly—after a few weeks, I had to spend a lot less time visualizing it pushing out all of my insecurities. Now, that persona was a lot more like an old, comfy sweater. When I needed her, I reached back into my head, slipping into the mindset in a matter of seconds.

I experimented with her personality nearly every day. At first, it was only while I was hidden away in my home, locked away inside the bedroom. But I began to now grow bolder. I started doing it at school whenever I could find a moment of privacy. I'd even considered bringing a pocket mirror around, but that seemed excessive.

The effects were strong and immediate. Peter's circle of friends absolutely loved the new *me*. They seemed to love just being around this thing that I'd cooked up in my head to cope—and, if I'm going to be totally honest... I loved being *her* around them.

Peter, though, was a different story...

"This isn't like you."

I continued chewing on my chocolate bar as I kept my sneakers propped up on the railing; I watched all the other students exiting the main building for the day. Peter kept his eyes on me as he bit into the top of his *cornetto* cone.

"I've known you a long time, Clara," he added after he swallowed a chunk of ice cream. "I've seen you happy and I've seen you depressed, and this is... *worse* than that."

"Dunno what you're talking about," I smirked.

He sighed. "You've never been anything like this. Sam and the others might not know any better, but I do." He shook his head in defeat. "Whatever you're putting out isn't *who* you are."

I felt the persona slide away for a second—in my head, I desperately grasped at it, pulling it back over me. "Could be, this is who I am now. Maybe this is who I *want* to be."

"I doubt that's true. I mean, I can't say that I've ever read a psychology book, but this *cannot* be anything like a healthy coping mechanism."

I laughed. "A *healthy coping mechanism?*"

"Sure, what else would it be?" He licked at his *cornetto*. "I know you were sad for a while there—even depressed. But I've *never* seen you like this. Hell, before that whole vanishing act of yours, you would've scathingly mocked damn near *anybody* who acted like this."

Well, that's probably true...

"Things changed," I forced a smile.

He didn't skip a beat. "It's a pretty big change."

I grumbled in my head. *If you can see right through me—maybe it was foolish to think I could get past you like this...*

"Fine then," I took another bite of chocolate. "Would you rather see me hurting—or do you want me to try and fake it till I make it? Because I'm getting better, Peter. I'm *feeling* better."

He looked at me for a while there.

"You've just got to be true to yourself," he observed.

I laughed at his cliché advice, waving at myself. "Peter. *This* is who I want to be. Did you really think that I *enjoy* going through the motions, struggling to get out of bed every morning? We've been over this, haven't we? You know better than *anyone* the kind of stuff I've got to deal with when I'm at home."

"Yeah, your stepfather's a piece of work."

"Of course he is. And he's been in my life as far back as I can remember. My sole guardian isn't related by blood—and treats me like I'm some *burden* that he's been saddled with." I had finally let my persona slip from my grasp.

I shook my head sadly.

*Don't you **dare** cry, Clara.*

"I just can't live like that. I could barely manage before I disappeared, but after what happened..." I let the half-eaten chocolate bar fall into my lap as I covered my face, holding back tears. "I need to be stronger!"

Before I realized what was happening, Peter had his arms tightly hugged around me. I felt myself slowly give way to his comforting, supportive warmth. "Hey, shhh..." My best friend whispered reassuringly, trying to calm me down. "It'll all be okay, Clara. I promise you."

I pulled my face from my hands. "You *can't* promise that, Peter. You don't have that kind of power."

"Try me," he smirked handsomely.

"Go ahead then. Make me forget."

Slyly smiling, Peter tilted his head. "That was kind of the intent. Come out with me again, and I'll try my hardest to do just that."

"No more movies," I insisted.

"We've only been to two in what, five months?"

"What, isn't that enough?"

He chuckled. "Well, what *else* is there fun to do in this ridiculous town?" He saw my face and added: "I'm certain I can probably figure out *something* we could do..."

I took a deep breath. "Okay."

"Okay *what*?"

"Okay," I nodded. "Try to make me forget."

Peter smirked handsomely. "Oh, I will, Clara. I don't

want you to have to fake being positive around me. I'll make you forget all about crazy vampires and castles, and whatever happened out at the lake."

It stung that he brought that up—more so that I knew he'd never believe anything about what really happened... but I couldn't blame him. The true story was wilder than whatever his imagination cooked up. He brushed my chin with the back of his knuckle in an endearing gesture.

"I want to make you happy."

My breath caught in my throat.

"I don't deserve you, Peter."

He honestly laughed. "Course you do."

"No, I mean..."

His eyebrow lifted. "What do you mean?"

My words caught in my throat again as I hesitated to explain things to him. After all—how could I? What could I honestly tell him? '*Well Peter, I'm sorry that I've been so mopey for months, it's just that... well, remember all those weird things I deliriously said when I was found? Remember when I was blabbering about a castle filled with pale, beautiful creatures that craved my blood?*

*As it turns out, that all **actually** happened...*'

"Don't have to say a thing," Peter confidently smiled. "I couldn't begin to understand what you've been going through—but I just want you to know, Clara..." Briefly, he took my hand in his. "No matter what happens, no matter what's going on in that head of yours, I'm here for you—so long as you'll have me."

"That's why," I smiled at him.

Peter furrowed his brows. "That's why *what*?"

"That's why I don't deserve you," I simply replied.

"Oh, that's nothing," he chuckled. Before I could ask or grow uncomfortable with his touch, Peter released his grasp on my hand. It was another classic example of why this boy honestly deserved my trust—and why he was the closest person I had in my life. I didn't even have to ask. He would make little gestures like that, but instinctively knew when it was too much—when I wanted him to stop.

*This world just doesn't feel like it belongs to me anymore. It's nice to have an friend here, even if it's only the one. But, if it had to be **just** one...* I smiled adoringly at him. *I guess it's nice to know I made my choice count.*

"See?" He laughed heartily. "Just like that. I want you to look like *that* when you're around me, Clara." Peering in my eyes with a squint, he added: "Unless you're faking it again, of course. Can't have that."

"Oh, of course not," I beamed. "Anyway, it'd be nice to get out of the house again, and Harold's been a little more agreeable lately. Maybe he's letting things slide."

"Yeah," Peter laughed. "Maybe so."

The adoring smile widened a little—but, behind it, I felt next to nothing. I *did* enjoy Peter's company, and all that he'd done for me. I believed every word of what I said to him.

And yet...

The emotions were too hard to feel from the darkest depths inside of me. Somewhere, deep down inside, I was pleased to see I could fool Peter after all.

Glad to see I've gotten better at pretending.

I'M NOT SURE HOW PETER PULLED IT OFF, BUT HAROLD was letting me out of the house again.

"You'd better be back before bed," he snarled before I could even ask. "I'm not going to wander around tracking you down if you go missing this time..." Harold sipped at his beer. "You hear me?"

"Yes sir," I nodded quietly.

"Good. Then go. Get out of here."

I didn't bother hesitating, even though Peter and I weren't supposed to meet for a few more hours. Eager to get back out of this horrendous house while opportunity still knocked, I dropped off my things in my bedroom and darted back down the hallway.

Halfway down the stairs, I paused.

I walked back up to the room and grabbed my extra backpack out from my closet. Checking it briefly, I noticed the spare clothes usually kept for my trips back into town. I snatched a few extra from my wardrobe and stuffed them into the zipper compartment, then slid downstairs.

Harold barely acknowledged me—I slunk past him and pushed my way out the door. I had decided to make my way towards the bus stop, but I wasn't taking the stop that Peter had requested.

"Back before bedtime!" Harold snapped after me.

"Yes sir!"

I PULLED MYSELF OUT OF THE LAKE WITH A SIGH.

The sun began to set over the abandoned park as I dried off on the shore, eyeing my backpack. Since I'd had the time free, I thought I'd make the most of it. Apparently, that meant flinging myself into a murky lake.

Oh well. It was worth another try...

Disheartened, I changed back out of my lake-stained clothes to dry off in the waning sunlight. While I let the shine bake the grimy lake water off my skin, I started to wring out the wet, miserable garments and laid them out on my spare towel to dry up a little.

Still doing this so late in the year was really starting to push it. I knew that I'd have to abandon this little hobby of mine soon—at least until the spring came. Besides a few cold days during a snap, this season had oddly been a warm one so far. It wasn't typical for late November to still stay comparatively hot in the West Midlands... and soon enough, I knew that hypothermia would *kill* me if I kept plunging myself haphazardly into the stupid lake.

Disgruntled about it all, I pulled out my cheapo phone; it was the replacement for the device I'd lost in my travels. The service out here was practically nonexistent—but that didn't mean I couldn't check the time.

What? My eyes bugged out.

It was **way** later than I thought.

I hastily shoved a disposable conditioner into my hair and ran a bottle of water through it. *Guess that I'm gonna look like a she-beast when he sees me, but at least it's better than smelling like a swamp thing...*

It might have been in a complete state of disarray, just like everything else in this lost place, but there were still serviceable lavatories nearby. Scooping up all of my damp swamp clothes and tossing them into the garbage, I went straight for the ancient bathroom and quickly scrubbed as much of the filth off me as I could manage in the sink. The water was freezing cold—to expect anything hotter than 'scraped off an iceberg' was frankly never gonna happen—but at least the park still had clean running water.

You take such good care of me, I thought to the park.

*Even if you won't—or **can't**—give me the one thing that I need.*

Once I'd done my fastest, quickest scrub yet, I changed into fresh underwear and gazed upon the slap-dash girl staring back in the mirror. For someone who'd just leapt into a lake a few times, I had to admit that she didn't really look *too* unsightly.

For a platonic adventure with a friend, it would do.

After spritzing on something to finish covering up any scents that might still be lingering on my body, I dressed in the set of mildly presentable clothes I had brought along. Glancing at the time once again, I started hurrying up.

That hair looks atrocious, I winced. *Oh well, I guess.*

The best part of cleaning up in the bathroom of an abandoned park was that I never had to worry about an audience. Hell, I'd only ever seen the caretaker who found me once during my trips out here. I wasn't sure what loose kind of schedule he ran, but he was almost never around.

Maybe he's in other parts of the park, I wondered.

It wasn't really that big of a place, so I didn't think that was terribly feasible. Regardless, I absolutely did not mind having the lake all to myself, and nobody seemed to care that this park even existed. As far as I could tell, nobody else ever set foot on the grounds. *It's sad to think about,* I frowned to myself as I scooped up my bag and made my way back outside.

Peter awaited a few stops over; it would take me half an hour to get back out to the bus stop—but I still had time if I hurried. I felt confident that I could make it.

My eyes trailed across the lake as I walked around it, ready to make my way through the gnarled walkways in the overgrowth. I thought again to how little anyone else seemed to care about Broadmoor Park, and it sent a fresh ripple of sadness throughout my heart.

Besides Peter, this place was my only friend.

It knew things about me that even *he* didn't—and, once upon a time, it had sent me hurtling towards my destiny... and yet, it was as empty as my heart. I shook my head in disappointment. *A place as incredible as* **this** *doesn't deserve to be so carelessly forgotten.*

I wasn't done with this place yet.

Little did I know—it wasn't done with *me* yet, either.

CHAPTER 11
ELLIOTT

I was already halfway through dinner when the doors to the great hall creaked open.

Kinsey and I glanced toward the noise to see who dared to interrupt my feast.

Nikki stepped in with a laugh. "So it's true, then."

I sighed. "What? Where the bloody hell have *you* been? It's been over a week since I've left the tower!"

"I've been a tad busy."

"Busy doing *what*, pray tell?"

"What you haven't." My sister took herself a seat at the table, not waiting for me to allow her the courtesy. "While you were up there playing *King of the Mountain* completely unopposed, I've been beneath the castle."

Ah. "That's right. You were studying."

She shrugged. "Somebody had to."

Kinsey glanced back and forth between us. "I don't think that I understand..."

Nikki smiled, obviously ignoring her. "So, what are we thinking, Elliott?" She pulled a plate over and snatched up a chunk of roasted elk, biting in. "Was it long enough?"

"I guess it *had* to have been," I leaned back in my chair. "By now, the rumors *certainly* have spread far and wide. While the vampire lords deal with their catastrophes, they must think me shattered and destroyed."

Kinsey eyed me curiously. "What *are* you talking about, Lord Elliott?"

My sister grinned even wider.

"Kinsey," I turned, "I have been sitting alone with you atop that tower for a *reason*. It's a strategy for beginning to deal with our enemies abroad..."

"Oh boy," she snorted. "*This* is gonna be good."

I ignored that display of impertinence. Judging by the amused, cat-like grin across my sister's face, **she** did not. "Until a few days ago, I've been up there since, well..." I hesitated, almost unable to spit out an answer. "Since the day that we sacrificed our best chess piece on the board, I meant to give them all an impression of weakness and loss. Global *complications* bought us more time for that."

"You... *wanted them* to think you were grieving?"

"I *was* grieving," I clarified in no small annoyance. "But it's true that I want them to underestimate me.

They will. It took less than a week for my entire hold to hear tales of an *otherworldly* guest within the castle... so I suspected that they have become long aware that the lord of Stonehold is a recluse in his own lair."

"But why?" She tilted her head. "What's to gain?"

"Besides brief pockets of time," I reminded my vassal, "you were artificially asleep for more than four months. What do you think I was doing with all of that time?"

She blinked. "I... I'm not sure."

Nikki grinned. "Elliott hasn't been *in* the castle."

Kinsey's expression grew stoic. She swallowed back a complicated set of emotions. "You... what?"

"The node in my suite lets me leave the tower unseen. I was free to come and go as I so pleased, so long as I began adhering to the regular schedule of Silas' visits."

"But... where did you go?"

"The training grounds."

Kinsey's mouth dropped. It was quite an amusing look on her. "The training grounds, Lord Elliott? Far up north on the island, past the mountains? Those court-yards have been long abandoned... who trained you?"

I turned to my teacher.

Nikki grinned sadistically. "While Elliott was 'sulking' in his tower, I studied all the lore I could get my claws on in the library. At agreed upon times, my brother and I took the nodes and met in the northern grounds, far beyond the prying eyes of civilization. There, we dueled. Every day."

"For *four months?*"

"Minus a few weeks," I added hastily. "I needed you pushed far enough to lose your patience *first*. Once you were spending most of your time asleep, and your waking moments furious at me, I knew the time was right."

I could tell she was hurt. I felt a brief pang of guilt.

"But... why?" She choked back disappointment. "Why risk yourself and hide it all behind my back? You made me your vassal to *protect* you. What's the point if you're just going to disappear without me?"

"Everyone in this castle knows that you are my loyal servant, and that you would never willingly allow me to endanger myself. Your presence in my chambers ensured that we remained undisturbed, and allowed my journeys to remain undiscovered and uninterrupted. You kept me safe in ways you will never fully comprehend."

"But I've seen you grieve," Kinsey looked confused. "Every day, you looked like a complete mess!"

"His heart wasn't in it at first," Nikki shrugged. "To be fair, neither was mine." She shot me a filthy glare— and I thought I knew why. "It's not that we didn't suffer. It's that we put our anguish to good use. We had to be ready."

"Ready for the vampire lords," Kinsey realized.

I nodded. "They will come. The challenges facing

their kingdoms will not last forever. I've played the part of the defeated, sulking lord in his tall tower, but my attempts to temper down expectations of violence can only go so far. Nikki has been researching in the oldest parts of the castle library, and we've been honing our skills."

"You've been drinking yourself into a stupor."

"I have," I begrudgingly agreed. Nikki flashed me a disgusted look; I pretended I didn't see it. "Flushing toxins from my system isn't a terribly difficult or time-consuming process for a vampire lord—and my body clearly classifies hard liquor as a toxin. I sober up quickly when I must."

"Huh. I didn't know that," Kinsey noted.

"There are a great many things that you don't know—and the vampire lords aren't exactly quick to divulge those potential advantages."

"You could have trusted me."

"You sound frustrated," Nikki grinned slyly.

Kinsey glowered. "It feels like a betrayal."

"It is not," I replied calmly.

"How do you follow? What makes that true?"

"The fact that I *say* it's true," I insisted darkly. "Kinsey, you have made a consistent habit of questioning me at all but every turn—behaviour very unlike a trusted guardian. I don't see how you can act surprised when you present opinions on every little move I make. I had to keep these choices secret, for your sake as well as mine."

I leaned in closer to her, ready to say what had been on the tip of my tongue for ages.

"I do not tolerate those who swear an oath and fail to trust me. It breeds concern, and it breeds a liability. I value your opinions, naturally—but you must *never* allow me to question your trust."

Kinsey blinked, but she didn't look afraid this time.

Good. I need vampires with **backbones** *around me...*

"You have my trust," she responded thinly. "Would you like another one of my opinions?"

"Speak," I replied quietly.

"Whatever plan you are setting in motion, the people haven't seen it," Kinsey retorted. "My Lord, all they know is that you sit up there atop your keep and issue vague, harmful decrees to solve their concerns. I've *heard* how you sound when Silas comes. You can tell yourself that this has all been for a better cause, but Lord Elliott..."

The far doors opened.

A string of servers came out with an array of food; they hesitated awkwardly when they reached the table. "My Lord," one said, "we weren't expecting more company."

"Not a problem," I shrugged offhandedly. My gaze slid towards Kinsey. "This one won't be eating tonight. In fact, she won't be eating for the next three days. She must learn that disrespecting my power comes with consequences... give her food to my sister here."

The servers didn't dare to question my authority. As they began dispensing entrée platters across the table, the former guard looked away from me, tearing up.

"Go back to sleep, Kinsey," I commanded her. "Make it a deep sleep, until I call upon you again, and no sooner."

She followed my order.

The servers left as fast as they could. It all but escaped my notice. Soon, the room was silent but for the sounds of scraping silverware.

"Wow."

My eyes cut to my sister. "What?"

Nikki smirked, taking a sip from the glass of blood in front of her. "And they say that *I'm* the cruel one..."

"Cruel?" I narrowed my eyes. "I disagree."

She shrugged. "The girl has a point. Even I can see that you've changed, Elliott. Can't really say that it's been for the better, either."

My voice took a warning tone. "Nikki..."

"You forget, but I've been around for some of those sessions with our boring old chancellor. You don't take the time to think about your choices anymore. Brother, seems that you pick whatever answer best crushes the problem, despite the potential implications."

"My choices have been saving lives," I insisted.

"Your choices have been *terrifying* people. It's not that I don't like that—because I do." Her wild, piercing eyes flashed with a tinge of wickedness. "But your paragon of virtue here certainly seems to disagree with that thinking. She thinks you've been becoming an unfit ruler."

I snorted. "And you don't?"

Nikki took a bite of steak. "I don't think that you've been *completely* fair, but I wouldn't fault you for it. Perhaps you've been a bit harsh, but I would have been far worse. At least you're making decisions. We're experiencing a bad season, and there is plenty of room for *unpopular* choices."

I turned to Kinsey's silent, statuesque form.

"Don't go soft on me now," Nikki smirked.

"She questions me. She deserves this."

"If she questioned *me*, I'd have her hung."

"Then at least we have *that* difference."

"Yes," Nikki laughed. "And that's why we both know I should *never* be left in charge of this place."

I took a sip of blood. "Oh, my beloved sister, there are *so* many reasons." I counted with my fingers, keeping my eyes firmly locked to hers. "For one, I stripped you of your birthright to the throne—which you deserved."

She sulked. "Yeah."

"For *another*, I'd have to *die* first. And since you're

only about a century younger than me, you would have a very long time to wait for that."

"Not unless I *kill* you first."

I let that guide me to point number three. "Beyond that, you are dangerously unstable."

"I thought that was one of my better features," Nikki replied with a grin. "But, to each their own."

"For somebody I trust in battle, it is beyond reproach... but if fate *ever* left you in command of Stonehold Castle, I can only imagine that the hold would be doomed to fiery destruction." It was incredible how quickly her eyes lit up. "Fiery destruction that *you* would bring, just to watch the world burn."

Her cunning gaze slid from my fingers to my eyes; out of her widened stare poured a kind of dark, sadistic excitement. I had hoped that my assessment had been wrong, but I could see just how much the idea appealed to her.

It sent a shiver down my spine. I repressed it.

"You know, you're probably right," Nikki conceded. "I don't want the throne, because I can't *trust* myself to rule. I'm aware of my... failings. But maybe it would serve you to take time to recognize your own? You could start by not punishing your most trusted allies. This little sweetheart is the only thing keeping somebody like *me* out of *your* big, fancy chair."

I sat back, taking amusement in Nikki's words, but

also giving them a moment to sink in before she continued.

"You *also* need to be thinking about some sort of heir to the throne—long before we have a succession crisis on our hands."

I almost spat out my blood.

"An heir?"

"Of course."

"Don't you think I'm a little young for that?"

"You're three hundred seventy-*six*."

"*Exactly.*"

My eye briefly hovered on Kinsey's frozen stare. I couldn't help but wonder what she'd think of this talk, as dutiful and steadfast as the former guard was—but at that moment, I remembered *why* I'd ordered her sleep, and I entertained my amusement no longer.

"We're not discussing this," I told Nikki.

"Clara would have come of age soon..."

I slammed my fist down on the table.

"Do not speak her name."

Nikki grinned evilly. "I knew it."

"Do not test me," I warned her. "Or else."

"Or else *what*? You'll simply order *me* to go to sleep, too?" Nikki smiled innocently. "Oh wait. You *can't*. They never messed around in *my* head, did they?"

"Nikki..."

"You can play it off however you'd like, but let us both

be honest here..." Nikki turned to my other vassal, frozen in time. "*She* isn't fooled..." Then she met my gaze with a defiant look. "And neither am I, brother. You *have* grown colder and darker in your grief. It's because of that little *snack* that you made me send away. She was the only one who ever trusted me, even when I put her in danger..."

"Don't you dare say another—"

"I wish I could say that it would be better if she had never arrived... but I can't, because she *changed* me. Not by much, of course."

"Not enough," I replied.

Nikki gave me a wicked grin. "Not *enough*, but Clara still made me a little better for having ever encountered her. Can you truly say the same, Elliot? Caring for her *ruined* you—now that she's gone, you need to move on and find someone to make a little baby Craven heir with, and well before those feelings of yours inside eat you alive."

I rose from the table. "Nikki... leave."

"All of this will have been for *nothing* if your broken little heart turns you into a monster. Maybe I'd be better in that stupid chair after all."

"I am *ordering you* to leave."

She rose from her seat as well.

"Don't worry, Elliott. I'm going."

My sister downed her glass of blood and sauntered off

away from the table. Before she was out of earshot, I heard her voice drift back to me in a singsong taunt. "Between you and me, I think I'd be ruling the kingdom the same way that *you* are... and I'm smart enough to know that's a ***dangerous*** thing."

I sat back down as the door closed behind her. As the minutes passed—startled by that implication—I found myself questioning absolutely *everything*.

CHAPTER 12

CLARA

"I'm thinking that it's about time you earned your keep, little *Princess*."

I glanced from my cold bowl of soggy oats.

Harold's cold, steely glare leveled at me. With a bite of crisp toast in his mouth, he didn't chew so much as gnash it sideways. Ever since I'd been found and refused to tell him where I'd been, he'd taken to eating whatever he felt like while providing me with little more than gruel.

My stepfather swallowed in irritation.

"Your keep," he repeated.

I turned back down to my oats and nodded.

"*Oi*," he snapped his thick, grubby fingers in front of my face. "You look at me when I'm talking to you."

I imagined then what it might be like to break the

bowl over his head. In my mind, I pictured the soppy, milky brown goop as it splashed across the table. Maybe he'd fall backwards in his chair. Maybe I'd scream.

Instead, I met his thin, angry gaze.

"Of course," I acknowledged. "What can I do?"

He bit his lower lip in a disgusting half-scowl as he stared into my eyes. Those dusty cogs in his head got to turning—they probably didn't get much use these days, and I wondered what kind of oiling they'd need.

"A job." He took another bite of his toast.

My spirits fell. I knew better than to grasp this as if it were an opportunity. As much as I loved getting away from him as often as I could, Harold had a nasty habit of taking everything good in my life and corrupting it.

In short: he made me hate everything.

"No need to job hunt," he smiled proudly. "Your old man already got you a little something lined up. Special. So that saves you the fuss of eating up my food another few weeks while you drag your arse finding work."

He leaned in closer. "Courtesy of the *boys*."

I couldn't bear to look at him. Harold's rowdy pack of mates, his *boys*, had brought me no shortage of grief for the duration of my life with him. They encouraged my stepfather's worst behaviour, chiefly by convincing him to drink well beyond his limits. They'd leave me to deal with the drunken lout in the middle of the night—and at his *most* belligerent.

"Speakin' of them, I'll be having them over tonight. It's our card-playing night."

"It's Saturday," I replied coldly.

"Eh? What's that?"

"*Saturday*," I repeated for him. I knew that he'd hate the tone in my voice, but I just couldn't care less anymore. "Your card nights are always on *Fridays*."

"Yeah they are," he chewed angrily. "But you were out with that boy last night, right? Gallivanting around town, yeah?"

I tried but failed to see the relevance.

"You weren't here to take care of us," Harold spat out. His tone told me this was somehow my fault—and that he'd make me pay. "So I rung up the boys. We all decided we'd play tonight instead. Moved our game night over to let you have a night out." I could barely understand him over the gnashed food behind his thick, oily lips. "Ain't that sweet of us? Moving our week around *you?*"

I nodded, fighting back tears.

"That's what I thought. So they'll be over tonight. I need this place spic and span by then—no good showing off a ruddy house, is there?—and we'll need you to be a good little girl and keep our drinks topped off."

He grinned wickedly, as if eager to provoke me.

"Of course," I nodded. "I'll take care of it."

"Of course *what?*" His grin faltered.

"Sir," I answered in defeat. "Of course, *Sir*."

Somehow this disgusting man, in his petty little way, figured out how to ruin even Peter's gesture of kindness.

THE REST OF THE AFTERNOON WAS SPENT THUSLY: cleaning the kitchen, mopping the floors, scrubbing the baseboards, hoovering the carpets, disinfecting the fridge, wiping down the countertops, dusting the furniture, airing out the rooms, reorganizing the closets, sweeping the front, and watering the plants.

In other words, it was a standard Saturday.

The first of the boys arrived around 6:30PM, right in the middle of eating a fresh bowl of corn flakes for dinner. I knew to abandon my food and take his jacket.

"Hullo, Clara," Rob smiled.

"Hullo, Rob." I helped him slide out of his jacket and hung it on the foyer coatrack.

"You grow prettier every week," he leered.

I frowned. "You look balder every week."

Rob instinctually touched the large, balding patch atop his leathery head. "It isn't!" He defensively replied. "I'm just wearing it different today."

"Ah." I looked away. "Silly me. Looks good."

"You think so?" He grinned lecherously.

I didn't have the patience for him. But he wasn't the

worst of them, so I nodded. With a few years on Harold, Rob stunk like cigarettes and even had a similarly tall, thin build. My little barb threw him off just enough to not try and hug me with his spindly, beige old arms.

I reminded myself of my old mantra.

Take every victory, no matter how small...

"That you, Rob?" Harold waddled into view with a roaring laugh. It was rare to see him in direct sunlight; it was a reminder of how disgusting the man really was.

"Harry!"

The two men threw their arms around each other in a revolting display of filth. Their intertwining stinks made me want to gag, especially trapped with them in a hallway.

"C'mon, c'mon," Harold finally gestured on.

I followed them towards the kitchen. With a glance at the countertop, I realized that my stepfather had already noticed and tossed out my bowl of dinner. *Typical.*

Harold and Rob sat down in the den, ready to swap stories from the week before. I was already making my way into the kitchen to pour their drinks when Harold repeatedly snapped his grubby fingers towards me.

"Waitress? Two cans of Guinness, now."

I ignored their raucous laughter.

Instead, I slid two frosted pint glasses out of the freezer and fetched a pair of cans from his ancient beverage cooler in the garage. Holding the glasses tilted as I poured the beers, I set the cans aside for recycling and brought them their chilled pints.

"Attagirl," Rob smiled hungrily. *I guess it's too much to ask that he look at the **beers** when he says that...*

My stepfather merely snorted.

It wasn't too long before the others started to show up. First came Gabriel—a portly, lecherous Italian man with bloodshot eyes, yellowing teeth and gnarled fingertips. At least in his mid-fifties, he sniffed repeatedly and had almost a permanent half-grin on his face. It widened when he cheated. Which was often.

Then came Benny, the oldest of the boys by a decade over even Harold. Never without a thin layer of grime, he always loved to tell the story of missing a major lice infection as a kid due to his hatred of the common bath. Skittish of soap even in his upper middle age, his natural musk was a combination not unlike wet dog and dust.

But the worst part about old Benny was his smile. He never quite looked at you when you had his attention. Instead, he looked just *past* your head—when that was matched with the big, dopey grin he carried so often, the effect was just unnatural enough to be unnerving.

Benny, surprisingly, was rarely inappropriate with me. But when he'd had a few beers in him, he got loud—*real* loud. It was loud enough that I could hear him even through the den's ceiling while I tried to sleep.

When he came in, he gave me a treat—a handful of gold-foiled Rolo chocolates to eat. "Our little secret, yeah?" He grinned in that unnatural, dopey way. "Don't go telling your dad, now."

"Th-thanks," I smiled weakly.

I'd have likely appreciated the gesture of kindness, had I not unwrapped the least melted one to find its smell just as rancid as his own. *How long were these things in his filthy freaking pockets?*

I brought him a cold beer and topped off the others. It was roughly around that time that Harold's final 'boy' showed up, my least favourite one.

"Hullo, Clara," Maggie flashed her white teeth.

"Hullo," I reluctantly greeted her. "Come in."

Maggie brushed me aside. "Don't mind if I do!"

The way that I was always told the story, she joined with the boys on account of her ironclad liver. Coming into town with her boyfriend—*a 'prissy little piece' and the worst three years of my bloody life*, she always recounted—Maggie joined Harold's pub group as they overheard her bragging about her liquor tolerance, got herself challenged to a shot contest, and then drank them *all* under the table.

"We've still gotta have a girls' night out one day," she winked at me. Her curled lip showed off the prominent golden tooth in her molars.

I hid a shudder.

She always pushed the rest of the boys to beat their standing records. When they started dropping out from drunkenness and she reigned victorious, Maggie started to show her true colours—and they weren't pretty.

"Do you want me to bring that in?" I asked.

Maggie looked down at the small bag in her hand. "No, this is a gift. For the house."

I knew what that meant. I didn't like it.

I took her coat and led her to the den.

"*Maggie!*" Rob and Benny called out in unison.

"Hullo, boys!" Maggie grinned widely as she took a seat with them. "Deal me in. I brought you a present!"

"Oh yeah?" Harold took a puff of his cigarette as he started dealing a hand of cards to her. He eyed the bag she set on the table with a greedy gaze. "Oh, what'd ya bring us this time, Mags?"

I walked into the kitchen to pour her drink, aware that there was no point in hanging around.

"Hoo-boy!" Benny chimed up.

"Mags, you've outdone yourself!" Harold laughed.

Gabriel whistled approvingly; his growl sailed my way. "That's the *good* stuff, too..."

I knew it, I groaned inwardly.

She brought everyone some expensive bottle of liquor. That meant I was gonna be up a *long* time tonight...

I COULD BARELY KEEP MY EYES OPEN ANY LONGER.

The hours had dragged by.

Thankfully, most of the boys were now passed out in the den. Since they were all staying the night, that meant breakfast for all of them in the morning—and Harold loved showing off to them just how far under his thick, grubby thumb he kept me.

They'd also made a disaster of the bottom floor.

Already spent all day cleaning, only to do it again...

Ground zero of the disaster was the den. Harold, in his most natural form, was drunkenly snoring away on the couch. Maggie sat half-asleep upright, idly watching the telly while Rob, Gabriel, and Benny were passed out in the chairs or on the floor.

This is disgusting, I thought bitterly.

It wasn't like I could even escape away to my own bed. Sleep offered me no peace anymore. I knew that recurring horrors waited in my dreams as soon as I fell asleep.

But I was exhausted.

"*Oi,*" Maggie muttered my way. "Another shot."

Everyone else was asleep; my patience with the night sat firmly at its limit. "You've *got* to be joking."

It seemed like she didn't hear me for a moment.

"Another shot *now*, Clara." Her evil, twisted smile

sent a shiver down my spine. "Or else I guess we won't get to have our *girl's day out...*"

Nauseated, I left without another word. I pulled one of the last clean shot glasses—but her fancy bottle of liquor was nowhere to be found. I eventually spotted it sitting on the kitchen table.

Fatigued, I sat down to pour the shot.

That was the big mistake here. Sitting down. There's no denying that. But I was exhausted, and the idea of just plain *sitting* was so inviting...

My head grew heavy as I reached for the bottle.

I felt my pounding heart.

Wait. Why is my heart rate so high?

It must have been for all the trees surrounding me. They *were* a pretty scary sight. Worse still was the feeling that I was being followed—no, *chased.*

I was running.

Aren't I at a table?

It didn't matter. Something was coming for me.

I ran as hard as my heart could handle it, desperate to put distance between my unseen predator and me. All of this seemed so utterly familiar, but I couldn't quite place my finger on it until—

I thought of Lorelei Craven and her advice.

I felt that I'd remembered it again, not too long ago.

The mother of the Craven siblings asked me about my recurring nightmare one day, walking through her private gardens. She even offered me a small suggestion when I explained the 'pinching' approach to dreaming. *"Learn how your palm feels as you run your finger down it. It's far subtler. Mimic that in your dreams, and see how the sensation feels."*

I wasn't sure why I thought of that then, as I sat at the kitchen table but ran through a forest. But I followed the advice, and I felt nothing.

Oh god, I realized. *I'm asleep again...!*

It should have brought me joy, knowing that I was not in any real danger. But becoming lucid hit me with all the memories of doing this, again and again.

I realized that I was trapped in the forest nightmare —and the malevolent force was coming for me once more, ready to rip me asunder...

I could already hear it splintering trees behind me. *If I stop running,* I thought in panic, *I will die. But* there was no escaping this thing. I was going to be slain here, again...

"Oi!" I felt my hair get yanked.

All of a sudden, I was at the kitchen table again. My hair was caught in Maggie's fist as she sharply twisted my head around. "You're supposed to be pouring me a—"

The bottle exploded.

The table cracked.

The linoleum tore.

Cabinet doors splintered.

The kitchen descended into utter cacophony—it was an eruption of wild, kinetic chaos that ended just as swiftly as it began. Everything ruptured and stopped.

And it all spread from me.

Drunkenly, Maggie released her grip on my hair.

"W-what on Earth?"

I looked at the insanity around us. It silenced itself just as quickly as it had come. There was no explaining what had just happened; I was stunned. Yet nothing else in the house stirred. *I know they're drunk—but how did all the others manage to sleep through* ***that?***

Maggie looked at me, her bloodshot eyes filled with a unique kind of terror. The room around us looked as if it had split beneath my very feet.

I turned to her in open rebellion.

"I'm going to tell those drunken bastards *you* did this," I demanded angrily. "And if you say a word, that'll be a *tenth* of what I do to you."

"What *are* you?" She muttered in horror.

"What *am* I?" I looked up at her. The words came to me out of the darkness of my mind, like something I'd heard a long time ago. "I'm a *witch*."

Maggie took a few quivering steps backwards before finally bolting from the kitchen. The sound of a door slam told me she'd wasted no time in abandoning the house.

I stayed seated in that chair at the cracked apart table, running my hand along the fractures.

Maggie had been scared.

But her fear had nothing on mine.

When all that chaos erupted, I felt it rise from a place deep inside... But I knew it wasn't me that had done this. Something from that place had pierced through the cracks of my waking sleep...

And it had just destroyed my stepfather's kitchen.

A NONDESCRIPT CHRISTMAS CAME AND WENT WITH MY barest notice—not that the holidays were ever fun with Harold around. The makeshift kitchen repairs had barely begun, and like usual, I was the one left cleaning up the mess.

Not that this mess was anything close to usual.

When my stepfather saw the damage he was *furious*— but Maggie's late night disappearing act made it all too clear who was responsible.

They all blamed the alcohol, same as they always did —and that spared me a great deal of anguish dealing with Harold. In one fell swoop, their dreaded card game night, the weekly bane of my life, was put on hiatus.

One week passed without it.

Then came another.

Soon, it was clear that they just weren't coming back. I started to think maybe disgusting old Maggie was the glue that held them all together. Now, their dirty little group was falling apart.

It should have made me happy.

But it didn't.

CHAPTER 13
KINSEY

The door slowly creaked open. Bent over the table in the war room, Lord Elliott studied a map and several stacks of sheathed documents.

I hated to see him like this. During the long reign of Lorelei Craven, her only son bore a logical and insightful mind... one that was almost *coldly* logical. I knew that he'd make a great vampire lord, even with some growing pains. But the cold and callous lord of Stonehold Castle had only grown darker and chillier as the months passed since the arrival of the human girl.

My eyes saddened.

The human...

Whoever she was, I'd never met her. She had been kept far away from the rest of us, allegedly to protect us from the mythical vampiric fixation on human blood.

From what I understood, royal guards were immune to its allure—probably something to do with the *treatments* they gave us. Three of our order were that girl's guardians, but I wasn't one of them.

Maybe it was better that way. I couldn't trust the girl who could twist my master's heart like this. My Lord quite obviously adored this human, because I'd never seen him embrace the darker side of his nature until she was gone. This was the man who saved my life when I was broken and weak. *And now, he is the same. Broken. Weak.*

He'd sent me above ground to face down one of the most dangerous creatures in the hold—a tatzelwurm. The creature was so vicious, so utterly terrifying that I *still* woke up in the middle of the night, clutching at the covers with a scream. It had been a last, defiant act in the face of death. I never expected to see him survive...

I'd saved his life. He'd saved mine.

We were bound together by guardianship.

All that I wanted to do now was lead Elliott Craven back away from the dark and gnarled path before him. But it wasn't my place—and I knew he'd never listen to me.

It broke my heart to see him suffer.

But it broke even harder to see that my master's actions had dire consequences. We lived in such dark and perilous times, but so many of his decisions seemed short-sighted in nature. If Lord Elliott lost his way *now*, only to lead us directly towards our own destruction...

I was duty-bound to enforce his will. The laws of my order were very clear on this. We served the vampire lord. *However*... a guard's service ran far deeper than that.

If a sitting vampire lord is deemed objectively unfit to rule, the allegiances of a royal guard are forced to change for the greater good of Stonehold—no matter the means. Survival of the bloodline was of the utmost importance, yes—but the people required saving.

The vampire lords watched the people.

And the lord's guards watched the vampire lord...

This was all the more complicated for me now that my master had made me one of his own vassals. Lord Elliott insisted that I was no longer a royal guard, but the ruler of the castle seemed blind to the conditioning applied to our order. There was some complicated psychiatry in effect. It was not so easy to simply *decide* to no longer be one of the guards, not really. And not for me.

I felt pulled in two directions.

I didn't know what to do.

Still standing at the door, I realized that my master had finally glanced up from his work. "This had better be—" Lord Elliott paused as his face settled into recognition. I held my breath, and he sighed. But I still held my ground, standing in the doorway and holding up a glass of blood with a quiet look on my face.

"Thought you could use a drink, Lord Elliott."

He nonchalantly waved me to the side.

"You should drink," I insisted politely.

"You can see that I'm too busy for that."

I sighed quietly, walking over and setting the glass down near him. "I can see loads of things."

He rolled my eyes. "Things like what?"

I hesitated, realizing my mistake. I regretted saying those words—but it was too late, and we both knew it.

"Out with it," he snarled, "if you must."

What are you becoming? I asked myself. *Why do this to yourself, my Lord? Can't you see all these things happening to you? What that means for the rest of us?*

His eyes narrowed. He expected an answer.

"I can see that you're barely eating, Lord Elliott. You're going gaunt because you've skipped blood meals— more than one. I can see how bitter and callous you've become over the past half a year. I can see how the subjects cower from you in the halls—and I can hear the things that they whisper after you pass..."

Casting me a glare, he replied dryly: "Is that all?"

"I can see many things. Those are the important ones."

He didn't speak, instead choosing to watch me.

My fears were building to a burning crescendo. I

knew that it was a terrible choice to make—one that would only anger him—but I felt *compelled* to try to reach out. The cold and calculating Elliott Craven was my master, and I just wanted him to get better.

"Lord Elliott..."

"Enough," he replied.

I'd already made up my mind. I ignored him. "You're not well. We can all see it."

"Not *well?*" He asked with dark curiosity. "Why, I can think clearly now, and I'm far stronger than I was when I first assumed the throne. Do not assume, Kinsey, that my health is in decline."

"The way that you've been *acting* isn't healthy," I dared to continue. "I didn't meet her, but the guards knew you were deeply fond of Clara, Lord Elliott. None of us ever fathomed that sending her away would leave this kind of lasting impact. Someone should have stepped in. It was a mistake to to send her back—I see that now."

"A mistake? He glowered. "She needed to be *safe.*"

"Things looked bad at the time," I conceded. "I look at the way things are now, and I see what her departure has done to you—and what it's done to this castle. I shudder to think what it's doing to the mainland..."

He snarled. "You are rapidly forgetting your place."

"I had to speak my mind."

"Then you will let me speak mine," Lord Elliott

replied coolly as he straightened his back. "Stonehold has never seen this level of *logical* efficiency, nor has it ever required it. This winter has been the harshest on record —yet we are surviving it. None of my subjects have starved yet, none of them have frozen to death, and not even in the deepest northern regions. When has this ever been the case, even in the mildest of winters? I am protecting my subjects. My priority has been to see every last one of my people live through the season... because if war *does* come to us, as I suspect it will, we may need every last one of them."

"But what about the future?"

He snarled. "What *about* it?"

"My Lord, your decrees have been saving lives—but at what cost to the hold? We're deforesting the North at a rate that hasn't been seen in millennia. You haven't begun any kind of rationing of food or supplies. The southern mines are straining to keep up with production demands. You're not even *moderating* the use of our chrysm stores."

"You will recall," he rebuked me, "that the creature we faced below the earth—the one that very nearly killed us—butchered half of that mining settlement before we even arrived. There is no reason to restrict the mining down in Gransome Village when they are already running at half of their usual capacity."

"It's not just that."

"Then enlighten me," he challenged me.

My voice rose. "Lord Elliott, look at the atmosphere in the castle alone! They all *fear* you! You've become a black plague upon the halls of your own citadel! These decrees only grow more loose and dangerous by the day! We may survive this winter... but what of the next? When disaster strikes five or ten winters from now, will we have the stores necessary to weather it? The decisions that you've made are hurting the hold! When are you going to *finally* take a cold, hard look at yourself, and realize what you are becoming with every new sunset?"

Placidly, he stared me down. "Are you finished?"

"You're ruling this hold with an iron fist, crushing it in your grasp. You've refused council. You're ruling by edict. You're too swift to lash out. Even now, you are attempting to silence someone who still *somehow* believes in you. If we continue down this path, you'll be nothing more than a cruel and heartless *dictator*!"

I'd had never raised my voice to him like this. For a moment, it took him aback. As I panted in frustration, I hoped I might have finally broken through to him. But it was for naught—his face turned almost to *pity*.

"Lord Elliott," I said. "I do not serve a tyrant."

He laughed. "I am *not* a tyrant."

"Not yet," I conceded. "But you *will* be."

"Well, if that's what it takes to get them all through

this season—if that's what it takes to survive the impending wrath of the vampire lords..."

I watched him with open regret in my eyes, feeling him slip further away. He was choosing his path now, and he was choosing *wrong*.

"Then that's what I will become, Kinsey. If I truly want to serve Stonehold, the *right* way, then I cannot allow such primitive emotions like *weakness* or *grief* to overcome me. We shall face the hypothetical dangers of winters to come when they arrive."

"Lord Elliott..."

"Clara is gone. Every accursed day, I must make peace with that. If you had met her yourself, perhaps you would understand the depth of my pain. In her stead—just as I predicted the very day I met her—this world hangs on the brink of open chaos. *Everything* changed the moment a human stepped foot in our castle." He shook his head, lost in his convictions. "There's no going back now."

"But we have an era of peace," I argued.

"For a mere moment in time. Stonehold's enemies are distracted as the forces of nature seem to conspire against us all. But this peace will not last for long. They're angry, Kinsey—and if the disasters grow at all in ferocity, they will become desperate. They will come for us."

"There has to be another way, a better way."

He *laughed* at me.

"I am trying to guide this hold through the long winter. Meanwhile, I'm desperate to keep the world at large from tearing itself apart at the seams. Every one of us shall suffer before the warmth is upon us, but we will survive." His voice lifted to a loud snarl as his fury burned. "With you—or *anybody else*—as my personal witness, I will *not* see this world drenched in fire with my own two eyes. If that means I must become, as you yourself say..."

He paused; then he spat my own word back at me.

"...A *tyrant*? So be it. History can make me its villain or its hero when I'm dead in my grave—in a world I guided away from the brink of destruction. I will do whatever it takes for the *greater* good, as is expected of me."

I turned away, unable to look at him.

"Judge me if you must, but you honestly have *no idea* what it's like to balance the weight of a thousand vampires on my bare shoulders. I feel the weight of their lives, their futures, and their *progeny*. For all their sakes, I must be strong. I cannot be weak."

It occurred to me then, as I listened to the rage of the vampire lord. "You needed her."

Lord Elliott gave me a venomous look. "*What?*"

"Clara." I spoke with dawning realization. "I can see it behind every word you speak. You *needed* her. Her place in your life kept you away from these choices. She was your moderating influence. Without the human, Lord Elliott..." My saddened eyes betrayed a sense of resignation. "I fear that you are doomed lead us into darkness."

Of course, I knew better than to use her name. My lord forbade that. But I had to punctuate my point with the sort of emphasis that only came with broken rules.

My heart swelled with fear as his eyes narrowed.

"I have no further need of you now," he replied.

I nodded softly and sadly. "Of course."

When I walked over towards the door, his voice came in a bitter command. "You are my vassal. I said that I have no further need. But I didn't say that you could leave. You will stay *here* as I so demand it."

I turned to face him. "This is what you demand?"

"It is."

There was no reason to argue.

Reluctantly, I took my seat nearby, against the wall. As I settled in, my eyes slid across the glass of blood that I brought in. It still rested in place at his side.

"You should still drink that."

"Go to sleep, Kinsey," Lord Elliott commanded.

I nodded, and then I stared into space.

CHAPTER 14
GARRETT

I was not very excited about the United Kingdom.

It was freezing cold, for one.

But it wasn't the same kind of bitter freeze sort that New York typically inflicted. England—as if purely out of spite—was buried beneath an unbelievably thick, wet chill that soaked down to the bone.

The cold here was *oppressive*.

I didn't find it matched my temperament.

As the personal assistant for one of the highest ranked executives in Clover Pharmaceutical, I did not get any say in where I lived, at least not for the moment. My prized, beloved Manhattan condo would simply have to wait for me—its calm, modern yet evocatively classical ambience left alone, useless to me for now, especially with its thirty-eight remaining monthly payments.

Perhaps if I'd taken a more *traditional* job, I would have never stepped foot in this chilly, soaking country.

But traditional jobs *bored* me.

Working for Vera Partridge? That was *never* boring.

Speaking of, the Devil herself climbed out the back of a private black sedan, red pumps hitting the pavement first. Despite the sunglasses, I knew she was narrowing her eyes my way. With the toe of my shoe against its leg, I slid a chair out for her.

"Your coffee, Ma'am," I waved to the sealed drink.

The cutthroat, diabolical Chief Operations Director of Clover Pharmaceutical marched several strong strides straight towards me and slipped into her seat at our small street-side table.

"How do I look?" She asked, uncharacteristically.

I paused, wanting to be accurate. "Professional."

In nuance, she tilted her head, eyes still hidden behind the sunglasses. I knew that expression. I'd better, at any rate—I was now coming up on five years serving beneath the infamously strict and fickle woman.

"Precisely the intent," she replied.

Mrs. Partridge removed the seal from her drink and lifted the coffee to her lipstick lips. She took a deep swig of the drink—a sugary sweet caffeine drink, because my boss nurtured her sweet tooth as if it were her flesh and blood.

"How is Birmingham treating you?"

I shrugged. "It's a city, I suppose. The waterfront is quite appealing at night. I've grown to appreciate a few of the classier restaurants in the area. There's a French place just up the way that has been taking fairly good care of my palate. All in all, not terrible." I pushed my glasses up the bridge of my nose. "For *England,* at any rate. Otherwise, I find this place to be rather boring."

"You'll manage, Garrett," she replied dryly. "I'd have liked to put you up in London, but it wasn't in the cards. Too remote. Too noisy. Far too busy for our needs."

"I'm grateful. London seems a terrible place to live."

She smirked, sipping at the coffee. "I'd have thought it better suited to your tastes, honestly."

"I make it down from time to time. There's a direct line to London from the train station you just came in through. I'm not quite convinced that I'd have enjoyed it, once the novelty finally wore off."

"You always find a way to surprise me."

For my first three years of working beneath her stature, Vera Partridge had rarely expressed any interest in my life outside of the office. She had little tolerance for making small talk—something I found agreeable. But then, as our careers became increasingly intertwined by necessity, my curt boss had begun to value my contributions enough to at least offer the *slightest* obligatory cordiality.

It wasn't expected. Refreshing, nonetheless.

Still, I was here on a mission. She had come here for an update on that mission; I thought it the wiser choice to cut the frivolities and get straight to it.

"Are we ready to work?" I asked.

My boss smiled, setting the drink aside.

"Project Layers is on track. Oversight has concluded, and the necessary arrangements have all been made. You'll find the European branch of Clover Pharmaceutical is now fully operational for your needs."

"Excellent," Mrs. Partridge replied. "Any news?"

"Regretfully, little so far. We have determined rather conclusively that the activation we discovered originated at the *United Kingdom* rift. Romania remains dead silent —but we've got echoes of the event recorded on two ground stations. We've monitored the countryside for readings."

"Nothing yet, then?"

"We *know* a rift is hidden here. We also know it can't be far away. We're ready to triangulate its source but, until we see another energy burst, it's almost impossible to pin the exact location. Until then, we wait, we read, we study."

I took a swig of coffee. Mine had already started going cold but, to be fair, I'd gotten a head start. "When the next passage happens, we'll be ready," I assured my superior. "We have teams prepared to mobilize."

We sat in silence for a few minutes.

Vera Partridge drank her coffee, dwelling on what little I had to report. I always offered straightforward responses without fluff or inflated expectations—I suspected this helped her personally select me as her private aide.

"It's interesting," she finally spoke.

"What's interesting, ma'am?"

My boss quietly gazed down the busy Birmingham street. Her large, opaque designer sunglasses still hid the emotions in her snakelike eyes from all else but me.

"For the very first time since the alleged Cataclysm, a traveler has completed a full cycle between both worlds," Vera Partridge responded with a cultivated air of sinister charm. "It makes me wonder if there is any *significance* to the timing."

"Significance?" I pressed my glasses up the bridge of my nose again. "Whatever do you mean?"

"Ah, forget it, then." she smirked thoughtfully. "Even in matters pertaining to magic, I don't tolerate such things as prophecies and coincidences. I should remember that I hold myself to that same standard."

"Well... it's certainly true that it was a faster cycle than we would have predicted," I offered her. "The first blip on our proverbial radar only took three weeks before looping back. The fact that it concluded so quickly is one of the reasons we took it seriously from the start, but to tell the truth here... I thought that it might have been a few *years* before the traveler came back."

"Probable that it's someone traveling from *our* world, then?" My boss turned back to me. I could tell that she was narrowing her eyes, even with the sunglasses. "Not the other way around? Do we know this for sure?"

"Eighty percent sure."

"Why not one hundred?"

It wasn't like Vera Partridge to ask questions that she already knew the answer to. I chalked it up to stress or excitement. "We've never had a full loop to study," came my reply. "We don't have any data to compare—only some scribbled notes, as well as ancient tomes that date back a thousand years or more. They're hardly gospel."

She didn't reply for a few seconds. "Of course."

"We do have clues, however. The seer's vision made it clear that it was somebody young—young and *definitely* human. At least, it was something *resembling* a human. The speed of the loop makes it unlikely that this was a freak event. The next time this traveler crosses between worlds—or another one comes, if only we could be so lucky to find a second of them—it should narrow our search range. I suspect that we'll have a solid grasp on the coordinates to that rift. And then we can predict and react."

"Let us hope they use the same one," Mrs. Partridge noted coolly. "We could have a serious quandary on our hands if this traveler starts utilizing any of the others. The last thing we need is to be cavorting around the globe, hunting for a ghost."

I leaned back pensively in my chair. "I'm banking on that being a non-issue. Call it a hunch."

"Oh?" My boss tilted her head at me again.

"When have my hunches been wrong?" I asked.

She didn't directly respond to that. "Regardless. As far as I am concerned, the timing is little more than strictly fortunate. Had this rift opened in, say, twenty or thirty more years, it's quite unlikely that I could capitalize on the opportunity at all. It would be my successor having this conversation, not me."

"Meanwhile, I would stay a long-forgotten footnote in corporate history," I observed. "Instead, I have a front row seat to the dawning of a new era."

"A seat you have earned," she replied in conviction. "I could not have asked for a better subordinate to bring into this vision. I sleep assured that you will continue to be an asset for the foreseeable future."

I knew what she was really saying.

You have earned my trust. Do not fail me.

"I have no intentions for anything less," I smiled with pure confidence. "I am eager to operate here as your proxy in the United Kingdom until the time is right."

"Oh, that won't be *chiefly* necessary."

I paused. "Is that so?"

"Correct," Vera Partridge nodded darkly. "Shortly, I'll join you here, conducting my business operations from the Birmingham outpost as well. On paper, I will be heading our beleaguered European market division. The truth is... I want to be here when that rift opens once again. I want to see it with my *own* two eyes, this time."

I didn't know if I was disappointed or not.

However, one question hung on the tip of my tongue —and I finally dared to ask it. "What if, for the rest of our lifetimes, we don't see any further readings out of the rift? It was quiet for so many eons. What if it remains dormant for the remainder of the twenty-first century?"

My superior seemed to consider that. She took another long sip from her coffee, then pulled off her sunglasses and stared me right in the eyes with a smile.

"Oh, but Garrett. It *won't* stay dormant."

"Do you know something I don't?" I risked a smile.

She set down her coffee. "Call it a *hunch*."

CHAPTER 15
ELLIOTT

The hard winter chill still clung to the air.

The season had been worse than predicted—and it left Stonehold Castle in a dark oppression. I didn't let it stop me; I was stronger now, stronger than I had *ever* been before. It felt rewarding to push aside such useless emotions as grief and loss. My mind was clear and ready for the task at hand.

Sooner or later, the vampire lords will come for us all.

And I have to be ready for them.

I knew that there were many in the castle who didn't understand. Some of them already tried to confront me; I would not be dissuaded from the path ahead. They would learn to understand, in time—or they would understand it best to *stay out of my way*.

There was only one I still questioned...

Standing in a hooded cloak with her back turned, *that* one was already with me—here, in the place agreed upon.

I ascended a couple of wide stairs, carved from stone, to the ancient tiled platform. Mountains surrounded the old Training Grounds on all sides. This place was buried at the bottom of a distant valley—far from prying eyes, and nearly impossible to reach without the single functional chrysm node connecting it to the greater Stonehold castle network. It made for the perfect hidden place to test your might and train in the combative arts.

Nikki Craven turned her hooded head.

Brandishing my curved sword, I whipped it around in swaying circles. She always chose to be defensive, ready to capitalize on any mistake I made; I knew that we'd be here all bloody afternoon if I didn't make the first move.

So I did.

Lunging across the platform at her, I held my weapon at point from on high. Knowing that a single strike from this blade was unable to kill someone with the blood of a vampire lord, I prepared to plunge the tip of this sword downward into my sister...

As expected, Nikki waited until the last moment.

The sword came down hard. She spun around in place and caught it against a large bangle smelt, from a material what we called Blackstone—it was a metal so tough, it was used to *sharpen* the strongest blades we could make.

The blade's edge ricocheted...

But I had struck her in this way over a thousand times before. I followed along the sword's momentum, twirling around to strike her again, and again, dancing backwards at a darting pace. My sister effortlessly took my rapid blows with both of her bangles—never losing her footing, even as she moved at a clear disadvantage.

"How painfully unoriginal," she teased me.

"Yet practice makes perfect," I grunted, jerking back a stride and plunged the sword forward once again. Instead of parrying, my sister effortlessly sidestepped at the strike and tripped me with a foot...

I rolled and skidded to a controlled stop, tossing the blade directly towards her. Enough power was behind it to force her to deflect it with everything she had; she had to glue her boots to the ground as she parried it upward and over her shoulder...

Which created the opening I wanted.

Before the blade even hit her bangles, I was up on my feet again and rushing straight towards her. As it clattered uselessly behind her, I launched out a solid punch directly towards her head.

Nikki dodged—*barely*—as she caught my flying fist by the wrist. In the same breath, her boot flew up in an arc to strike my own skull; I stopped it with a sudden lift of my forearm, barely absorbing the blow.

In seconds, we were hurling punches and kicks at one

another that neither could land. We twirled around each other in a dizzying duel, using nothing more than chaotic strikes and sweeps to try to destabilize the other.

Dodging my fist again staggered her; her striking boot swept me off my feet, but I landed on a palm and leapt back to my footing as her second kick followed, trying to knock me down to the hard stone.

Over months of rigorous training, she and I hardened our own bodies to absorb *countless* physical blows. At first, we had needed to be careful—all it would have taken was a broken bone and a visit to the medical bay to destroy the lie of what we'd been doing the past six months. But *now*, we confidently struck at each other with everything that we had; in the truest sense of the phrase, she and I had grown disciplined enough—now, *strong* enough—to fight each other to the point of exhaustion.

Thanks to intense and constant dueling, it was a supernatural kind of endurance, significantly strengthened.

Our wrists and forearms caught, deflected, redirected, or absorbed endless blows from limbs strong enough to crack stone at full strength. The dilapidated training floor bore the brunt of our exercise with fractures and breaks far more recent than the moss and weathered façade implied.

The sun began to wane in the sky as Nikki caught my

downward kick and flipped me onto my back. Rolling over before her heel struck my throat, she broke another tile as I spun up onto all fours and lifted my curled fists in a defensive stance.

Nikki and I straightened our backs.

"Stalemate," she noted with a smirk.

"One more hour," I demanded as my lungs burned. "I nearly had you that time, and you *know* it."

"Could say the same," she shrugged, wiping sweat off her brow with a lifted wrist-cuff. "No point anymore. We're evenly matched. We could be out here until the sun rises next, and there'd *still* be no clear winner..."

I cricked my neck, finally relaxing. "Fair enough."

"Besides," she licked off a little blood from her lip. "We promised, *one more*. That's it. Now that you've returned to the castle, it's much too dangerous to come back out here. It's pointless to sneak here if everyone *sees* us, yeah?"

"Consider it a birthday present, then."

"Birthday?" She tilted a head. "What, *today?*"

"That's right, my little sister," I smirked triumphantly. "Today marks three hundred fifty-nine years old. Perhaps another fifty years or so, and I get my second equinox."

"Don't you remind me. I much *enjoy* looking like I'm the older Craven," Nikki sourly frowned. "Hell, when you start aging again, I might *never* catch up with you. What if my equinoxes are earlier than yours?"

"What if they're later?" I countered.

She put her hands on her hips. "It's a shame they're so random. It'd be rather nice to keep up this trend, yeah? If you could just look older than me for, I don't know, the sixty or seventy years it takes me to eclipse you again..."

"Think of how *I* feel," I chuckled.

"Yeah, well..."

"What?"

Nikki shook her head, laughing. "I've got nothing. It's your birthday, then? Are we making a big deal out of those now, or *what?*"

I hesitated.

"Shall I sing you the song?"

"No," I snapped.

"Oh, calm down," my sister squinted an eye angrily. "If a simple thing like a *birthday* is gonna remind you of her and get you all twisted in a wad, then I'm not sure what to do with you anymore."

I considered snapping, but I held my tongue. "Not my fault that she happened to have a birthday while she was here on our island. What are the odds that our little human would turn seventeen years old in the short time that she was with us?"

"*Seventeen...*" Nikki repeated thoughtfully.

"I know. It's bizarre, isn't it?"

She grinned evilly. "Just makes us all sound immature by comparison, doesn't it? Humans age so strangely. They die, what, *ten* times faster than us? And yet... they develop so much faster, both mentally and physically..."

"Speak for yourself," I dryly replied.

Nikki pulled down her eyelid and leered at me.

"Case in point. You do my arguing *for* me."

"Yeah, well..." She noticed the old, forgotten sword on the ground a few meters over and scooped it up in a grip. "The memories are all we really have to remember her by. The sooner that you put her in the past, the better. We sent that girl on a one-way trip. The way that she told us, there *isn't* any magic on her world." Nikki flicked her curt gaze to me, her face settling into a embittered frown. "So, don't get your hopes up, I guess."

She held a sword, but her words twisted a knife.

"It was an interesting custom, what she taught us."

"What, the birthday thing?" Nikki asked, reminiscing. "Yeah. I liked the part with the cake."

"The song *was* a bit strange," I chuckled.

"A cake, a song, some *presents*... leads me to wonder why us vampires ever let the tradition go to waste."

"Probably because the healthiest of us all see a *thousand* birthdays," I reminded. "You truly wish to be subjected to that kind of blatant, egotistical display—so many times in the rest of your lifespan?"

"The way I remember, it wasn't like that."

"Enlighten me."

"Well, she called it a *celebration* of mortality. It was

just an excuse to get a bunch of friends and family around to swap stories and... oh. I guess I'm seeing a problem here."

I frowned. "We don't really *have* friends, do we?"

Nikki froze in thought. "Guess not."

"This is a lonely life we have."

She looked at the blade again. "Yeah. It is."

When her eyes met mine, I could sense the twinge of sudden malice in her heart. *What a surprise,* I thought to myself. *I wondered how long **that** would take...*

Without any provocation, she swiftly hurled the sword straight at me with a powerful flick of her wrist. The only move that I made was a sharp arc of my forearm; I caught the weapon by its handle—merely two months back, that kind of force might have broken the bones in my grip.

"Nice catch," she smirked with a devilish glint.

I merely sighed. "Nice throw."

Turning over my shoulder, I hurled the sword into the distance, about as hard as she'd thrown it at me. The blade flew in a straight arc, piercing the ground behind.

"So, what do you think?" I asked, turning back. "Could I face a vampire lord in hand-to-hand combat?"

Nikki shrugged. "I think you need a second opinion."

"I'm not interested in picking a fight just yet."

"Not what I meant..."

"Right," I sighed, shaking my head. "*Lorelei.*"

"You know... **wherever** she wandered off to, I suppose I kinda figured our darling *World Champion of Motherhood* might have sauntered on back by now..." Nikki growled. "Didn't she say *anything* about where she was going?"

I thought back to one of the last conversations I'd had with the apathetic former ruler. At that time, I was barely recovering from a tense duel with one of the most vicious wild beasts that Stonehold had on offer—the very same monster that nearly ended Kinsey's life, as well as the lives of my accompanying guards. That's when Lorelei Craven came to me for a serious conversation, telling me all sorts of half-mad craziness that I barely recalled and didn't give much attention.

I'll be leaving soon, she'd told me.

But she never said where, or that it was for any longer than a few days. Her tone led me to think this was a short sabbatical—by now, I was starting to think it was worse than the former vampire lord had led me to believe.

"Just that she was heading for the mainland. For all I know, the infernal woman is dead."

"That'd be a shame," Nikki noted calmly.

Of course, that wasn't true at all. The ascended blood of the vampire lords roared in my veins. I would have felt it the very *instant* she passed on—likewise, all the others.

I felt bad, suddenly.

Neither of us had spent a lot of time discussing what had become of our mother, and I couldn't leave the castle unprotected to go and seek her out. At my request, Nikki stayed nearby to study and train.

In our own ways, my sister and I had spent our time preparing for what was inevitable—but it had never really occurred to us that our mother might *never* come back.

*What if she **needed** us?*

"Lorelei has been increasingly erratic over the past few years," I replied coolly, dismissing the thoughts. "It could be for the best that she abandoned the throne—even if she threw me under the wagon as she did so. Wherever that daft woman has gone... either she's fine, or she'd criticize us for wasting time fretting over her."

Nikki smirked. "Yeah, you're probably right."

I had my personal reasons for sparing our mother very little love, but it was something of a disappointment that her last living daughter could so easily make peace with it. *The only other sane one ever in our family is dead and buried...* I sighed burdensomely. *Now, I find myself surrounded by lunacy—a twisted, demented sister, and a darkly aloof mother off **who knows** were...*

As if hearing my thoughts, Nikki snapped me out of them with a clasped hand on my shoulder. The downward drift of the sun behind her only underlined the dutiful frown on her face.

"We've been out here too long. Let's head back."

I sighed. "You're right. Someone will be looking for us soon, if not already..."

Nikki and I fell into step together as we descended the stone steps, making our way towards the abandoned, broken buildings that circled the training grounds.

A few of them still served a use—stockades of weapons and armor, half of which we had further worn out in our months of diligent dueling—but one of these old buildings held the chrysm teleportation node that led back to our castle, far beyond the horizon.

As we stepped into the husk of four barely-standing walls, ostensibly for the last time, the node flickered to life near our presence. Nikki and I walked into the red glow together; it began to thrum under our boots.

She smirked. "Oh. Before we go. One last thing..."

"Yes?" I asked, annoyed.

"Happy birthday, brother."

I snorted, hiding my approval. "Thank you, Nikki."

CHAPTER 16
CLARA

One night in late February, as the dream forest rose into existence around me, I realized that I wasn't running for my life this time. This wasn't startlingly new to me anymore, not after countless months of experimenting with this amulet on.

But there *was* something different.

There stood a shape in the distance. The shadows from the forest canopy disguised it beyond a faint silhouette, but whatever it was, *it was staring **directly** at me.*

I froze in place at the sight of it.

"...Elliott?"

The shape didn't move.

I took a few tentative steps forward; I thought better of that and began circling towards it. As I'd feared, the shape seemed to turn its head to follow my path...

*Maybe **that** is the killer in my nightmares,* I gasped.

"Who are you?" I shouted defiantly.

I heard it chuckle, but nothing more.

The way I saw it, I had two options: approach the thing and figure out who it was—and what it wanted—or turn back the other way and bolt until it was gone. Something told me it had a purpose for being here tonight, and some part of me was worried I might never see it again...

"Don't be a coward, Clara," I told myself.

Summoning up every last ounce of courage, I chose the only move that made sense—I squared my shoulders and marched straight towards the silhouette, refusing to let my conviction waver.

The closer that I came towards it, the more detailed the shape became. The shadows seemed to slowly melt away as the dark figure stood motionlessly on the path ahead, content to merely watch me approach. It was the moment that I stepped out from around the closest thicket when I could finally see who—or *what*—it was.

The manifestation was hunched on a cane. Dressed in bohemian wraps, an elderly woman warmly smiled at me.

And memories began to start sliding back.

The woman appeared to be quite amused with herself. As she watched me step closer, she laughed ever so lightly. "You made the right choice, Clara. I wondered."

Suddenly, I remembered who she was.

"Grandma?" Perplexed, more than a little surprised, I was taken aback. "What are *you* doing here?"

"And what a way to greet me!" She smirked in victory. "I'll let it slide. Good to see that you *do* remember me."

I paused. "Why *wouldn't* I remember you?"

"Well, when's the last time you saw me?"

I reflected on that for a moment. "When I was a kid, I think? I don't remember that far back all that well..."

She shook her head. "Oh, my child. You've seen me a lot more recently than that."

"Grandma... what are you talking about?"

Her grin widened as she hobbled closer on her cane. "I see that you're wearing the gift that I brought you. It could only follow you into this place if you wore it all the time; it seems that the Blackwell Amulet is finally binding to your spirit." Her face grew warm with joy. "It's been a long time since it has tasted magic. Oh, my darling, you're doing it. You're saving that old thing from a slow death—and it is slowly rewarding you in turn."

I glanced down at the amulet.

The amulet is binding to my spirit?

"Oh, don't fear it," Grandma gently smiled. "That is an artifact of great power, or at least... it is, in the *right* hands. Once upon a time, it belonged to me—as it did with *my* grandmother, and hers before her. That pretty little trinket goes back, oh, *quite* a while, I would imagine..."

I didn't have a lot of time to study the amulet now with freshened eyes. My grandmother began to wander off in the opposite direction; I fell into step beside her.

"You said that I've seen you recently," I spoke. Without having to desperately flee through these trees, or fear the sudden emergence of the invisible predator, I found that I was bathed a strong sense of comfort I hadn't experienced in a long time. It was surreal to feel this safe again—more so in a place like this. "How could that possibly be true?"

She hobbled with her cane. "Do you remember coming to me in your dream state, Clara?"

I thought back. My memories were still awakening, in the back of my head, but that *did* sound kind of familiar... "I remember that... I think there was a spell," I answered tentatively. "But not much more than that."

"I need you to think *harder*, Clara."

It seemed an impossible request. I paused and focused on the memories. Grandma stopped, casually waiting for me to make the connection, as if she had all the time in the world. Of course, here in this world locked deep within the pits of my mind... maybe we *did*.

"There was..."

I furrowed my brow, pulling back things from what felt like so long ago. "There was a... *spell*, to make me safe... from something terrible. Vampires, I think. But something went wrong." The rest of it began to come back to me, and I gasped. "When I woke up, they told me I'd slipped into a coma for days."

"That's right," she nodded with a smile.

"And I remember..."

There was a flash—a distant beach beneath a full moon where no colour shone. I was there all alone. No. Wait. I *wasn't* alone. There was someone coming toward me—

"Grandma?" I blinked at her.

"Yes. That is the place where I still exist," she nodded, prodding at the sticks beneath our feet with her cane. "I brought you there to teach you what you must learn."

I shook my head. "I can't remember any of that."

She chuckled. "Of course you can't! At least, not yet, you don't. No matter how real that it was to you—and believe me, it was *very* real to you—your body itself slept. To your mind, you were in a dream... and we so *scarcely* remember our dreams over time, do we Clara?"

"I guess not."

The old woman shrugged. "We have had this little chat before. Oh, I knew then that you wouldn't remember any of it. I even told you as much."

I scratched my head. "This amulet..."

"Yes?"

Recognition filled me. "You gave this to me."

Amused, she nodded her head as she cleared a path in the brush with the tip of her cane. "I did."

"How? Why?"

My grandmother grew pensive. "When we dream, my child, we think of ourselves as seeing things in our heads. We sleep, we envision, we picture... But we are ignorant of a greater force in play—one that we visit only in our sleep. There is a *connection* in our dreams that we can access—" She turned back to me with a knowing smile. "Some of us, of course, access more than others."

I followed her down the cleared path.

"And this connection..." I began to ask.

"I reached out to you through it, leaving you with what some might call an impossible gift. Not that it was easy, mind you. There are distinct rules to things of this nature. It took you so long to find me again..."

I remembered something else.

It was one previous night that I'd fallen asleep, a night when one I'd been jerked awake from the nightmare—and the force that chased me blew our kitchen apart...

"If I brought this amulet out of a dream, back into the real world..."

"Nothing says this world can't be real," she chided.

"Then... I guess, the *physical* world?"

"Ah. Yes. Much closer."

"Then... can *other things* be released from this place?"

My grandmother hesitated. "That is quite a dangerous proposition, Clara. What is it that you would like to *take* back out from your dreams?"

"There was another time when something almost broke through... a force of nature attacked me. Someone jerked me awake. I felt it chase me across the gap between *asleep* and *awake*. It nearly split my kitchen in two..."

"That is different," she replied. "Tell me more about this *force*. Do you see it often?"

"Every time that I sleep, Grandma... or at least, that's how it was until I started wearing the amulet to bed. Now, it only comes *some* of the time."

"What does it do?"

"It comes for me. It *destroys* me."

She was stoic. "How long has it been doing this?"

"Since a few weeks before I met the vampires."

Grandma chuckled. "*Vampires? What,* **that's** where you were? Blimey! No *wonder* it was so difficult to find you again, sweetheart. That does explain a few things..."

"It's terrifying," I continued. "It chases me across these very woods. At first, Elliott was there to protect me—just like in real life, when I met him on his vampire world. But ever since I was sent back home to mine, he's been gone from my dreams..."

Grandma shook her head bitterly.

I realized that I didn't recognize this part of the forest, although it didn't look much different than the rest of it. On a subconscious level, maybe I'd seen so much of these stupid trees that I instinctively knew there was something unfamiliar about them.

"*Precisely* why I hate magical trials," my grandmother shook her head. "What are you supposed to do with them without the slightest context?"

"*Magical trials?*"

She sighed. "You thought that it was coincidence? You started having the *exact* same dream, always with the *same* impossible enemy, right around the time you experience magic for the first time?"

"Honestly, I haven't figured much of this out."

"No, I can see that," she sardonically chuckled. "It's really your fault. You've been thrown into great things, my darling granddaughter, and they have ensnared you now. I fear you will have to deal with that dream until you best it, or until you lose your affinity for the arcane..."

Her eyes drifted to the thing around my neck.

"Why did you give me this amulet?" I asked her.

"Do you remember seeing it in your past?"

"The last time I saw it, or you, it was around *your* neck. You were wearing it."

"That's right," she agreed. I realized that she wasn't using her cane to smack a way through the brush anymore as our footsteps took us along a winding path in the trees. "You were a little sprout way back then. I figured that you might have the potential, but I wasn't certain."

"The potential?"

"Aye," she nodded. "To be a witch."

"A *witch?*"

"Cor! You haven't remembered *any* of this, have you?" Her shoulders rattled as she laughed heartily. "I knew you were always a heavy sleeper, Clara—but gods almighty! Next time, I'd better have you take notes!" She settled into a scowl, but her kindly eyes told me she didn't really mean it. "Yes, my child, you're a *witch*. **That's** why you have that amulet. **That's** why you have passed between the worlds, my dearest. But this is wrong, all so very wrong..."

"What's wrong?"

She sighed. "You've gone back too *early*, Clara! It's all those rotten friends of yours, the ones who put you into the coma! Their foolishness put you back where I could find you. But now, they've gone and tampered with things they fail to understand..."

"What are you talking about?"

She bitterly stamped the cane against the hard ground. "I gave you the Blackwell Amulet to charge it back up! I didn't know where you'd wound up, but I saw the *strength* of the magic flowing around you! Our family heirloom was *supposed* to soak up enough of that magic to manifest your latent powers. It could have taken no time at all! But now that you're stuck in our world with only the slightest trickle of magic left to absorb, it's going to be much more difficult to get back to where you *belong*."

"Wait—" I stopped us on the path.

She turned, a sly grin on her face.

"Grandma—are you telling me ***I can go back?***"

"Of course! *Of course* you can go back!" She heartily laughed. "Why, you've already crossed the gate between the worlds twice now; did you really think they could shut the door behind you for good?"

The revelation stunned me.

Elliott, I thought with rising excitement, but my sudden well of hope turned to despair. "The lake," I remembered bitterly. "Grandma, I've tried to go back, time and time again—but it won't take me."

"The lake?" She waved the notion away. "You must be referring to one of those rifts of our world. You interfered in someone else's work as it took you across the worlds. Sure, that place holds immense power, but simply *showing up* and throwing yourself into a dirty old lake isn't gonna do the trick!"

"*What* will, Grandma?" Frantically, I almost grabbed her by her colourful garb. "Please, I've got to know!"

The elderly woman frowned, glancing to the amulet.

"That fancy piece of jewelry around your neck knows

where it *truly* belongs. It craves magic—and if you found it in a realm of vampires, then I'm sure it desperately wants to get back there, just as much as you do. But my child, I'm afraid that, well..." She met my pleading gaze with a wry frown. "With our heirloom drained of its great powers... you might just have to take the *long* way around."

"The... long way?"

"Yes," she noted. "And it won't be easy."

"Oh." I felt crestfallen.

"You will get there, Clara. But without any access to a direct source of magic, the amulet will need time to restore itself." Sympathy filled her kindly old eyes. "My darling, you might be trapped right where you are for a long while. Hell, if you're *truly* unlucky, it might even be *years*. Magic in our world is in *such* short supply these days."

Years? That thought was too hard to bear, and I felt a strong despair rise from the bottom of my heart.

"I have great confidence in you, my dear. You will find your way back to him, this... *Elliott* of yours. No matter how long the journey—or how long you must suffer the passing time meanwhile. You have *started* something now, and it's bigger than you. ***Much*** bigger..."

"What do you mean?"

"The cogs have begun to turn, Clara. Nobody has ever crossed between the worlds and made it back.

Without even meaning to, you've done the impossible! Of course... now that it *has* finally happened, I fully suspect that great and dangerous things lie on the horizon."

"You make it sound like I'm stirring up trouble."

"Why, you are," she chuckled.

"But, why *me?*"

Her eyebrow arched. "Oh, it never had to be you."

"It didn't?" I blinked. "I don't understand."

"The stage was set a very long time ago, my child, just *waiting* for the right sort of person to come along. Others tried to start it early; all have failed. Just look at that gypsy you told me about last time we met. You wandered into the wrong place at the wrong time. She was likely *never* going to succeed in her plan, whatever that might have been... but then you intervened. And that set the wheels in motion. And now, this train's left the station..."

I remembered how terrifying meeting that woman had been—and how angry she was. "I didn't mean to."

"Of course you didn't. But you did, and so here we are. If everyone meant to do everything that they did, I suspect that the world would be a very boring place, dearie..."

"But *you're* here," I reasoned aloud. "I saw Elliott in my dreams for weeks, long before he and I met. How can you say that these things aren't related? How can you pretend I'm not *meant* to be here now?"

"If you are to *truly* inherit that amulet I've bestowed upon you," she replied unhelpfully, "I suppose you'll just have to solve these mysteries yourself. Won't you?"

We fell into silence together, continuing down into the trees. It was surreal to see all of this with another spirit nearby—and distinctly *without* the darkening threat of my impending destruction.

"So. What do I do now?" I asked.

"That's rather open-ended, now isn't it? What do I look like, some kind of fortune teller? Plenty of leaves around; should I consult them in tea? Perhaps break out the tarot?"

"If I want to see *Elliott* again. What should I do?"

The old woman briefly reflected on that question with a kind smile across her face. Her bohemian wraps waved around her old body in a wind I couldn't feel.

"I have already told you that the amulet needs time to regenerate. There's no telling how much magic it drew in while you were cast between worlds—but it's got nowhere near enough power for the kind of trip *you* want to take. If you can find lingering magic in your world, you can speed things up. Until it is strong enough again, you'll just have to have patience. Don't take the amulet off. Let it become a part of you; give it time to recover. That's the only proper way to cross back over."

"You think I can do this? Even without real magic?"

"I think you can do great things, Clara. The road ahead to becoming the witch you're meant to be will be hard, but very worthwhile. I think you'll be capable of something so extraordinary, it defies explanation. With you empowered, and that amulet at its full strength once again..."

She took in a deep breath of air.

"Oh, it'll be *magnificent*."

CHAPTER 17
ELLIOTT

Fighting each other to a standstill in high-stakes combat wasn't the *only* way I dueled my sister.

While we waited for the inevitable attention of the vampire lords, there were ways to hone each other in mind *as well* as body. As it so turned out, they didn't even involve having to slink away from the castle, like sneaking prisoners trapped in our own home.

Nikki Craven lifted a rook and took my pawn.

I moved a knight to jeopardize her king.

"Check."

She tilted her head, drawing her arms close around her legs while she sat perched across from me. It was quite an interestingly calm look for her. "You can't do that."

"Sure I can."

"No." She pointed to my own king. "No, my bishop is in line. You're putting yourself in check."

I followed her logic. "You're right."

I moved my knight back and slid forward a pawn to threaten her bishop. She shifted it back a step. I chased, and she ultimately took out my rook in a sacrifice. I added her bishop to my set of taken pieces—most of her army was off the board.

To be fair, that was equally the case for me.

"You've grown brutal at this," she grinned.

"I like to think I've gotten better."

"Not better," she clarified. "*Brutal*."

I grimaced. "I'm not sure I follow."

"You used to **never** sacrifice your pieces," she observed as she moved a pawn forward—one of the only two left on her side. "Now, you'll meet me in combat at every possible turn until we've whittled our pieces down to nothing."

"Do you not like that style?" I teased.

"Are you joking?" Nikki challenged one of my final pawns with one of her own—I took *hers*; she took *mine*. "I love it. Such bloodshed."

"I guess that I'm not surprised."

"Well, I mean. You shouldn't be."

After this massacre, the battlefield left between us was left random and jagged. My army was down to only five pieces—she had four, but the advantage was hers.

I lowered a glare her way.

My sister grinned teasingly, dancing past my rook and jeopardizing my knight. "You know... it's been a very long time since we've played this game..."

I went after her piece. With a swift move of my fingers, my rook claimed her pawn, only three steps away from my side of the board.

"We hadn't seen very much of each other since the accident," she grinned evilly as she left my knight alone and put my king back into check. "I stayed in the medical bay at first. After we spoke that day, I didn't remain on the island for long."

"Yes." I studied the board. "I remember."

Nikki shifted in her chair, propping up her cheek in her splayed palm while resting the elbow on her knee. "Do you now? It was *such* a long time ago..."

"Well, you wouldn't respond to anything for a couple of days. It was like you were *there*, but you really weren't. You stared without seeing." Pensively, I leaned back in my seat as the memory resurfaced to the forefront of my mind. "It was horrifying to see you like that."

Nikki nodded, her face against her palm. "Everything was still working itself out of my system."

Reluctantly, I moved a pawn. I already knew the game was lost. It was a vain move, sacrificing my pieces to keep my king alive for a few moments longer. *If the time came for us, would I treat my subjects the same? Would I toss their lives away to breathe just one more hopeless breath, if it meant ending the ones who attacked us?*

"The magic?" I said, shaking away dark thoughts.

"Yeah, the magic," her eyes drifted away thoughtfully, only to snap back just as quickly. "But it wasn't *just* that. What I had **done** warped me."

I paused. "We don't have to talk about this."

"It's been over a century, Elliott," Nikki rebutted me in a dark, defeated tone. "We've *never* talked about this. If not now, brother, then when? *Ever?*" Her eyes locked to mine; I felt a surprising fury burning behind them. "Would you perhaps prefer *never?*"

The game was clearly abandoned.

"Whatever you'd like," I answered dismissively.

"No," she hissed. "What do **you** want?"

"Do you *really* want to do this?"

Her face lit up with an evil smile. "Sure."

"What do you want me to ask?" I demanded angrily, sliding back into my chair. "Want me to ask you what it's like in that twisted head of yours? Should I ask you about hunting the deadliest magical beasts in the hold, just for a sporting death-wish?"

"Go *darker*," she grinned wickedly.

I snapped. "What, did you *enjoy* killing our sister?"

As soon as the words escaped my lips, I trembled with wide-eyed horror. I turned away.

"That was low. Even for me. I'm sorry, Nikki."

"Yes," she replied in a monotone.

I sighed, glancing back remorsefully.

"But you misunderstand," she continued with a deeply sinister grin. It unsettled me. *Hard to reconcile the sweet kid sister I grew up with against this seasoned hunter before me...*

"I don't follow," I said tentatively.

"Yes, you do. You know you do."

It took me a moment.

"What are you saying?"

"I'm saying that I *enjoyed* it."

My vision started to waver. "Nikki..."

"In the moment, at the very least," she recalled. "To feel that kind of magic surging in my veins—magic that I have resisted my entire life. To finally let it all free..." Her gaze slid to meet mine. "You can't fathom how *liberating* that was. That power rushed across my entire body. I felt it flicker in every nerve. It raises my heartbeat just to think of it. Brother dearest, I've never felt more alive..."

"Stop," I warned her. "Don't get like this."

"All my life, my body was a cage *filled* with magic. The only thing that it ever wanted was to be free. Mother had me train as child to restrain it, but that only forced up a mounting tension that bubbled inside, hungry, waiting just below the surface..."

There was no stopping her now. I could see that in

her eyes—the way she turned, her mind drifting a kilometer away in an instant.

"Did the killing make it stop?"

Nikki smirked evilly, but I could see welling tears.

"One problem solved, traded for *another*."

I SWEPT INTO THE ROOM. I HAD TO SEE HER.

Fiona lay unconscious in one medical bay room, where we hoped our strongest that she would wake up. My eldest sister, however, was not who I was here to see. There was nothing more they could do to save her, the nurses told us; it was all in her own hands. Fiona Craven had to find the strength to come back to us on her own.

In the next room over, the younger sat motionlessly, just as she had for days. Already, I could tell this day would be different. Just as the servants had told me, Nikki had awakened.

My beloved little sister turned as I pushed through the door, halting myself in the doorway. Something about her expression made me instinctively pause.

"Nikki? Are you... are you okay?"

"Of course," she blinked. "Come here."

I pushed my conflicted emotions down and crossed the room in the blink of an eye. Our arms wrapped around one another as we collapsed into heartfelt embrace.

"I feel like I should apologize," she muttered.

Her strange word choice astonished me enough for me to chuckle reflexively. "We'll worry about that later, Nikki. I know that you couldn't stop yourself from hurting her. We can figure this all out when she wakes back up..."

"That's not what I meant."

Something in her voice alarmed me.

I pulled back from my sister, just enough to look upon her face—and my terror immediately made me regret that decision.

*The contorted expression across Nikki Craven's face would haunt my darkest nightmares for **decades** to come.*

I was unable to look away.

"Why are you...?"

I didn't get a chance to finish that thought. Before I could react, her forehead smashed into mine. I floundered back from her medical bed in a daze before I hit the ground.

"Nikki—"

Clutching my forehead, I lifted my eyes to see her standing before me. Glaring down upon me with an insane and homicidal grin, my sister didn't move an inch further.

"It is so good to see you again, darling brother..."

There was a face approaching the door.

It was one of the nurses—but I didn't have time to—

Nikki turned and flung out a hand, arcing a burst of magic that hit the door and sent a web of wild cracks dancing along the impenetrable glass walls. The force flung the approaching nurse back to the floor and melted the hinges.

Getting out of here was no longer a simple affair.

I rose to my feet, a hand still clutching my head. "What are you doing, Nikki? What's gotten into you?"

She turned back to me, bristling with rage.

*"It would be so **satisfying** to shed your blood..."*

My jaw clenched. Whatever had happened to her when she attacked Fiona, it clearly still held her in its thrall.

"I'm stronger than you," I insisted.

Nikki diabolically laughed. For a moment, I thought I could hear another voice, layered beneath hers...

"Fiona was weak... and so are you."

"Our older sister isn't weak," I insisted. "Nikki, she's one of the strongest vampires in the hold."

*"And **how far** did that get her... in the end?"*

The question made me freeze. My gaze drifted over towards the damaged walls. On the other side, I knew Fiona Craven lay in that bed, fighting for her life.

"Control yourself, Nikki," I ordered her.

"Why should I?" She tilted her head, lifting a palm. "It is so much more fun to let it all out..."

*"Because you're **better** than this."*

Nikki took a step closer. "I don't want to be."

*"It's not up to you," I replied as calmly as I could. "We have a duty to protect this world, you and I. In time, Stonehold may be mine now... and if **I** fall, you will be its sworn protector."*

*She screamed defiantly. "**Screw the hold!**"*

"This isn't you, Nikki!" I moved my hand from my forehead. The pain still throbbed, but I had to focus on her. She needed me

now—regardless of whatever madness was going on in that head of hers. "Fight this corruption! Come back to me!"

Roaring with power, my sister hurled her hands to her sides in a scream. The air crackled between us; I thrust myself against the cracked glass—**hard,** feeling my bones shift out of place. The room filled with a vicious green fire that threatened to consume my flesh in a burst.

I'd seen magic before. I was no stranger to it.

But **nothing** like this. **Never** like this.

As I snarled in pain, the wall gave way. I collapsed into the hallway in a cry of anguish. Shattered glass pressed into my flesh as I lay against the floor, panting. I could feel it cutting into my skin from every angle. I wasn't a vampire lord; my veins had the blood, but not the activated magic—and all of its benefits. These wounds would heal once I plucked them out, but I knew the shoulder would need hours to recover. I also knew I didn't have the energy to pull myself up from the cold, hard stone.

My eyes drifted to Fiona's room. The two nurses standing over my sister had their eyes glued above me; it barely registered that the machines spat out a flat-line with a thousand little codes and warnings.

It was too late now.

Fiona, my beloved older sister, lay dead.

I felt myself being tugged up from the floor. Nikki crouched against me, pulling me into a hard, sudden embrace. Against the rain of her pouring tears, I became aware that my younger sister sobbed into her hug, holding me as close as she could.

"*Elliott—oh gods Elliott, I'm sorry!*" *Heaving with anguish, her tormented cries rolled out of her body like the bitter tears. "I can't believe I nearly... I can't believe that I..."*

She was back—and I feared Fiona's death had a part in it.

Despairingly, my chin sank to my tortured little sister's shoulder. Lifting up the good arm, I held Nikki close; I watched as our terrified mother shoved into the medical bay, surrounded by royal guards and nurses. "No matter what happens," I told my living sister, "I love you."

"How **can** *you? After what I've done?"*

My skull rested against the side of hers. "It's not your fault, Nikki. You couldn't control yourself. I know you didn't mean to attack us, either of us... and I need you to know that I love you." I held her as tightly as I could, ignoring the pain radiating from my wounds.

"I... I love you too, Elliott."

She was swept away and interrogated, ten minutes later. But our embrace in the chaos of the medical bay was the last I'd see of her for a hundred years.

❀

"Did you ever make peace with it?" I asked her.

Nikki smirked deviously. "With what?"

"With the corruption inside you."

She tilted her head, deep in thought for a moment. I could see the cogs in her brain turning as she considered my question. "Probably better to say that I learned how to manage it."

"How did you figure that out?"

Her expression darkened with her smile. "The trick is to *indulge* it, darling brother. My madness needs to be fed, or it will build up until it overpowers me again."

"Is that why you hunted the creatures?"

"Can't a girl hunt a monster for the pure joy of it?" She laughed airily, as if we were discussing something tamer than hunting vicious beasts. "It was rewarding, Elliott. But you're right—it did satisfy my need for bloodshed. Few things bring me the kind of ecstasy I find in chasing and hunting something that can kill me right back, if I'm not careful. Fighting them honed me into a more cunning creature—it made me far better at stealth and reconnaissance."

"Yes, I've heard some about your conquests," I noted. "A vampire deep in the wilds, moving from settlement to settlement and hunting the fiercest monstrosities our hold had on offer." I watched her eyes hold back the slightest hint of a sly, proud smile. "You became a legend out there. I always knew it was you. A lesser vampire wouldn't have lasted a week, let alone a *century*. You took down fearsome creatures that would strike fear into anybody, regardless of the blood in their veins."

Nikki couldn't contain the grin any longer.

"They had a name for you, if what I heard was true,"

I smirked happily. "I believe that they called you She-Who-Fights-Monsters." I leaned closer, lifting up an inquisitive eyebrow. "Otherwise known as The Bloodraven."

"Yeah. I never really cared for names."

"You wouldn't give them another. The storytellers did need *something* to call you."

"Of course I wouldn't!" Her eyes took on her familiar devilish glint. "I mean, could you imagine? The princess, disappearing into the woods with a pair of daggers and doing battle with the very wilds themselves?" Nikki shook her head. "I didn't need the attention. Nor did I want it. I was perfectly fine to disappear, and to become just another footnote lost to history... until I heard that we had a *human* among us. Then, I changed my intended destiny..."

I wouldn't let her small slip-up soil my mood—but I found myself suddenly eager to steer things away from that painful barb deep within my heart. "So, Nikki. If you *feed* the madness, you can *control* it?"

"It always sings to me," Nikki smirked distantly. "Even now, the whisper suggests that I run a knife through your heart." I didn't react; she very nearly looked disappointed. Nikki clarified her thoughts. "But it's not like it and I are two dueling minds, fighting over the same body. Maybe one time we were, a very long time before. It's all just me in here now—my demented madness and me, both bound together for all eternity..."

I took a moment to absorb what she said, feeling the weight of every word.

"Did I let you down?" I finally asked.

Nikki laughed. "Elliott, I *abandoned* you. I left all of this in my wake and disappeared away to keep all of you safe. There was *nothing* that you could do for me, not really... no, brother. I was beyond help. Even yours."

"And now?"

"I know what I really am," she replied as calmly as I'd ever seen her. "I am a monster and a *liability*, but I will stay by your side for as long as you'll have me. Besides... I get the feeling that sticking with you just might provide me with *prey* far more satisfying than any beast."

"It is dangerous to keep you on the island," I conceded. "There are plenty of things that you have done already to strain my forgiveness."

"Harsh," she muttered. "But probably true."

"But I *do* forgive you. And I *do* have faith in you."

Nikki hesitated. I could see conflict in her eyes.

"What is it?" I asked.

"It's just... it's funny."

I lifted an eyebrow. "What's funny?"

"Well..." Nikki looked at me oddly. "The things you're saying to me now. They're strikingly similar to the final words that Clara Blackwell ever said to me. Maybe you've left your mark on each other after all."

I felt my body stiffen into place.

Before I could curtly respond to that, Nikki looked over the near-abandoned chessboard between us. Her fingers shifted her piece across the board, sending a pawn flying.

A wicked grin spread across her lips.

"*Checkmate.*"

CHAPTER 18
CLARA

The school semester flew by at a breakneck speed.

The days themselves blended together in a constant, homogenous flurry. There was nothing to distinguish one from another anymore.

I fell into an endless routine.

I attended school, barely going through the motions in everlasting boredom. It barely even mattered that my education was drawing to its close. Soon, I'd be thrust into the post-secondary world, but could I ever truly adapt to a *normal* life anymore?

Disappearing back into my persona helped the time fly. Becoming a co-pilot to my own body, I let my more perfect self pull me through the utter malaise of my life. Even if that meant the days and weeks continued on without me, I could stomach the compromise.

The only thing about this I *didn't* like was the sense that I was constantly waking up. During the days, I sometimes snapped to alertness and realized I had little idea of what was happening around me. Running through the motions sort of does that to you, so I could only blame myself.

But it was so very *comfortable* to let my mind wander in relaxing bliss for a while, letting some imagined version of myself take the lead for awhile.

ONE AFTERNOON IN LATE MAY, READY TO STUDY FOR the latest tests, I took a seat beside Peter in the library.

As I did so often now, I comfortably slid back into my imaginary self like an old sweater. That girl filled my veins and flooded my body with brimming confidence. When I smiled slyly, she beamed out through my eyes.

"You look better rested these days," he noticed.

"Yeah, I've finally been getting quality sleep."

"Oh?" Peter scrunched his eyebrows curiously. "Guess that the nightmare's finally stopped, has it?"

"No, not quite that," I shrugged, pulling out my stack of homework. "But it's under control. I think I've had to deal with it so often, I've just... gotten used to it."

Peter bit the corner of his lip, studying me.

"What is it?" I asked, smiling warmly.

"You've been different lately. Even more than usual."

"Different?" I tilted my head in concern. "How so?"

"You know..." He bit the tip of his pen for a second. "I understand that things have been rough on you since they found you—and that Harold's been difficult..."

"Yeah, well. He's been manageable lately."

"You think so?"

I pulled out my homework. "Enough to get by."

Peter studied my eyes for a moment, but went back to working out math problems in his notepad.

After a few minutes of working side-by-side, he set his pen down. "You know, it's been nearly a year." He leaned back in his chair. "A year since you went missing, I mean."

I put on the flashiest smirk I could, trying to hide how painful that realization was. "Yeah. Time flies, I guess."

"We should celebrate."

"Celebrate?" I felt a pit in my stomach.

"Yeah. Celebrate that you got back, safe and sound."

"What, with pizza or something?"

He glanced off, chuckling to himself. The gesture was a handsome one, and it highlighted some of Peter's best. "I was actually thinking a little *bigger* than that."

The colour drained from my face.

"Peter, wait..."

Every word came out in a new burst of reluctance.

Why are you doing this to me? "Look... I know that it's been a while since we've hung out, and you've been amazing, but that's not the kind of step I'm comfortable making—"

"No, no, it's not that," he shook his head.

"Oh." I blinked, popping my head back.

"I'm asking you to prom."

My mouth went dry, but I couldn't tell if that was a good or a bad thing. The emotions were going haywire in my mind, and I couldn't settle either way.

"You want to... go to *prom* with me?"

He leaned in a little closer. "We'll be eighteen soon, you and me. This is our last year of school before we traipse off to uni. Not only that, but we can celebrate the anniversary of you being here... being *safe*. It's off by a month or two, but I call it close enough."

I fought the turmoil in my head.

My persona didn't *do* turmoil.

Classically, Peter could clearly still read my expression. "If you're not into it, then we don't have to. I just thought it might be a good idea to get you away from all of, I don't know..." He waved his arms around. "*This*."

"*This* is secondary school," I reminded him. "The same place where *prom* happens."

"No, the prom's going to be off-site," he grinned at me like he'd just beaten me in a round of cards. "The faculty picked a cozy little hotel ballroom as the venue.

It's not the newest or best, but from what I hear, it'll do the job."

"You want to go to *prom* with me?" I asked him again.

"I'd love to. It's settled then."

"Wait—" My whole body twitched, processing what had just happened between us. "That's not what I meant, I mean, I was just clarifying that you—"

"Then tell me *no*," he chuckled.

His tone told me one thing. His eyes said another.

This meant something to Peter Tatham. He wasn't just asking me as some sort of joke, or as something to pass the time. He legitimately *wanted* to do this—and he wanted to do it with *me*.

"You know we're not dating," I lowered my face.

He kept his eyes on mine. "I know."

"You know I'm not your girlfriend."

With a laugh, Peter nodded. "Yeah, I know."

"Then what... what do you want to get out of this?"

Peter's shoulders bounced as he laughed aloud, his eyes rolling as he took in a deep breath. "I don't have any kind of ulterior motive here, Clara." He glanced back. "I just think this might be what you need... and hey, I sure as hell don't need my arm twisted to take a beautiful girl like you out for the night."

"Do you really think I'm beautiful?"

Peter scoffed lightly—handsomely.

"Don't laugh at me," I insisted.

"I'm really not sure how you still don't see it." Peter spoke with complete sincerity, the kind that you just can't fake—unless you're an amazing actor, or one of the worst backstabbers in the world. "*Of course* you're beautiful. And you don't need me to tell you that."

My head shook slowly. I must've been looking at him like a deer in the headlights. "You can't mean that."

Peter took his hand in mine.

"I do," he replied softly.

"I don't know what to say."

"Then don't say *anything*, not just yet," he shrugged noncommittally. "I don't want you to feel *obligated* to come with me. I'm really not looking to try to drag you through something you're not ready for."

I put my other hand over his. It felt good to hold it between my own, even if it set off a bizarre sensation, deep down into my gut.

"I'm not saying *no*. I need to think about it."

Peter smirked. "That's all I'm really asking."

WHEN I CAME IN FROM SCHOOL, I HEARD SHUFFLING from the mostly-restored kitchen. Harold was typically passed out by now these days; I was disgruntled that he was up.

Unwilling to deal with him just yet, I tried to dart towards the stairs. *If I can just make it to the—*

"Oi!" His voice called out from a room away.

My breath caught in my chest. "Yes sir?"

"C'mere. Now."

With a heavy sigh, I reluctantly turned back from the salvation of the staircase. I dropped my things off on the edge of the sofa on my way. Before I even made it through the threshold of the kitchen, I could hear the greasy sizzle of whatever grub he was frying up.

Standing shirtless, Harold had his back to me. It was rare that I was subjected to the various pockmarks and boils on his back, and I was disgusted at the sight.

"Have a seat," he grunted over his shoulder.

Fearing the worst, I did as I was told.

He ignored me for what felt like forever. While my stepfather focused on whatever one-star cuisine he was whipping up on the oily stovetop, I sat there at the table wishing I'd at least brought a book. The only sounds were the various sizzles and pops of his cooking. At one point, he cursed as the crackling oil popped a few stray specks onto his portly stomach.

I'd have sighed, but he would have heard it.

Finally, he splattered a few things onto a plate and dug around in a drawer for clean cutlery. Satisfied, he poured himself a glass of juice while I hung onto every last little motion, trying to deduce why he might have demanded I sit and watch him cook.

Harold took a seat in front of me.

I expected him to start talking.

To my complete lack of surprise, however, he chose to start eating instead. I sat quietly and tried to not watch this disgusting pig of a man as he scarfed down a quarter of his plate in a minute.

He said: "I'm going away for a while."

I almost didn't realize he'd spoken. "Sir?"

Harold made a sickly smacking noise as he slurped up a slimy chunk of egg. After he washed it down with a sip of juice, he wiped his lips with the back of his wrist and cut into his bacon. "Going away for a bit, I told you. Got a bigger check this month."

"You're taking a vacation?" I was dumbfounded. It had never actually occurred to me that Harold would entertain the notion of a day spent outside these walls. I thought his idea of a vacation *was* this life—watching telly and bossing me around every hour that I wasn't at school.

"Looking after you, all this time? Course I am."

I wasn't sure what to do with this information. On the one hand, I knew that he'd never dream of taking me with him. On the other...

Isn't a little distance from him its own reward?

"Where do you think you'll go?" I feigned interest.

"Gonna visit me mum and me brother in London," he snorted, crunching into his overcooked bacon. "See me old pals down there, too. Real friends, yeah. Not like all these gutless scraps up here."

"The boys?"

He made eye contact with me for the first time since I'd come in—a filthy glare. He slid his thick tongue inside his cheek, licking up stray oil. "Don't talk about them again."

I nodded politely. All things considered, he seemed to be in a better mood than usual. "Yes sir."

Nodding angrily, he crunched into yet another brittle chunk of bacon. "Leaving in just under a month. Gonna be gone a week, maybe two." Harold lowered his glare upon me. "And I'll be expecting you to make use of the time and keep this place in ship-shape, yeah?"

I couldn't believe my good fortune. "Yes sir."

He smirked. "Writing you a chores list. Can't have you getting lazy while I'm gone, yeah? See to it that *everything's* done— or I'll tan your bloody hide raw when I come back. We clear on that?"

"Crystal clear," I nodded.

Never taking his eyes off me, Harold bit into his toast and slowly chewed. After swallowing, he nodded. "Glad you see things my way. Now, get back out of my sight."

With polite restraint, I let myself up from the table and scooped my things off the sofa.

"Oi!" He called out from the dining table again. "And don't you forget to come back down and clean this mess up! You don't live here for free!"

"Yes sir!" I grinned, flying up the stairs.

When I was back in my room, I dropped my things off on my desk and dug out the student calendar. *I have to be sure. There's no reason to get excited just yet...*

There.

Staring me in the face was the school prom, sitting just a few days into Harold's vacation. *If he's really going to be gone a few weeks, I'll probably have time...*

I reached for my phone, but I hesitated.

A flood of emotion ran through my head. It was true I wanted an excuse to *actually* enjoy myself. I didn't know what Peter really wanted to get out of the night out...

You trust him, I reminded myself. *He's your closest friend. Don't you deserve a night to just forget about everything and hang on his arm a little? What's the worst that could happen?*

Then, there was my dream diary. I lifted it from my bedside drawer, flicking to a bookmarked night—the most important entry that I'd written in that thing.

My grandmother hadn't returned to my dreams again. I knew she wouldn't, or at least couldn't. I didn't want to strain the amulet to try and call her back—not if I needed it to find a way to bring me back to Elliott.

Ages, she'd told me. *Maybe you'll wait years.*

Well, it had certainly been months. Ever since that

first painful day back here, it had taken *everything* within me to move on from my experiences in the vampiric world. Long before she gave me the news that I could find a way back, a simple truth had stared me right in my face...

I was frozen in time here. I knew it was true.

In so many ways, I had been unable to grow past it all. *If I pulled back, maybe it would be easier to get back to him...* Reluctantly, I knew the first part of that sentiment was to finally release this stubborn, iron grip that Elliott Craven still held over my mind.

If you love them, let them go... right?

Assuming that it really *would* be years... I just couldn't stand the idea of being stuck here in this mental place any longer. It drove me insane to feel all the longing, all the despair. I had to do *something* to break away from it.

A tear slid down my cheek. *I'm sorry, my beloved Elliott. But I can't cling like this to the memory of you any longer... It's killing me. I have to do to you what I did to Peter when I was on your world... I have to let you go to survive.*

I took a deep breath and lifted my cheap replacement phone, thumbing it unlocked in my palm. Unreasonably, it felt like a powerful moment—one of those defining ones, the ones that are so important you can instinctively *feel* them prepare to change your life.

I found that I was afraid.

But there was no reason to feel fear. I should have

felt relief at pushing Elliott back—at compacting down all my thoughts of him into a cardboard box, buried deep back there. But something in the back of my head stirred, and it didn't really seem like it was just nervous jitters.

It felt stronger than that...

You're being crazy, I told myself. *You'll be fine.* Before I could change my mind or allow the sensation to stop me, I flipped to my contacts list and dialed him.

Peter picked up on the third ring. "Hullo there."

My throat swallowed. "About that prom thing..."

"Yeah?" I could tell that I had his attention.

"Let's do it. I'm in."

CHAPTER 19
ELLIOTT

I stood at the edge of Lorelei's prized castle gardens. Everything was coated in white; even the sturdiest of her flowering plants was buried under frost.

My vassals stood at my side as I folded my arms.

"This isn't good," Nikki observed.

"No," I shook my head. "No, it's not."

Kinsey apathetically glanced over the horizon. "Is this kind of thing still going on in the other holds?"

"According to Silas, nature has run wild."

She frowned mirthlessly.

Ever since her failed little outburst in my war room, Kinsey's behaviour struck me as particularly broken in spirit. *If that's what it takes for her to quit defying me at every turn, then so be it.* "I guess it's no wonder the vampire lords have remained as silent as they have," she observed coolly.

"Maybe I was wrong, then." I sighed, studying all the frost. Never in the recorded history of Stonehold had a winter season persisted like this—*Why on Earth is there still snow in early June?* "Maybe I've been wrong about them all this time, and all of this preparation was for nothing."

"Wouldn't *that* be a crying shame," she snorted.

I didn't bother acknowledging that.

"That would be hard to believe," Nikki shrugged. "But still, it's unlike them to hold off like this. If I didn't see it with my own eyes, I'd never believe it."

I fully agreed with that sentiment.

My life as a vampire lord had taught me that the others were all bitter, backstabbing rulers thirsty for territory and power. With Mother gone, the time to strike had arrived. A young lord is always challenged for his throne...

Until now. *What if I've been handling them all wrong?*

It was trying times like these that I utterly detested our mother and her inexplicable absence. Even accounting for her uselessly fleeting grip on morality and patience, I was willing to turn to her for whatever aloof advice she might have to offer. *So long as she actually **did**...*

"I never figured out what was wrong with her."

Nikki glanced my way. "With who?"

"With Mum."

My attention flicker over to Kinsey. "You served

under Lorelei Craven during the final century of her rule. What light can you shed on the changes in her personality?"

The former royal guard thought for a moment.

"I'm not sure what to say. Your mother used to be such a caring and benevolent leader, but in the last half of my tenure under her... it had always been such an honour to be among her castle guards, but towards the end..."

I frowned into the distance. None of that helped.

"Makes me wonder if she knew something."

"Hmm?" I turned back to her again.

Kinsey blinked. "Lady Craven had such unending fire in her heart. She was indomitable in spirit and personality. Something took all the fight out of her. Maybe she knew something that we don't."

"Something that we don't," I wondered aloud. "Well, it's certainly true that she was always harping on about the *Sanguine Ones,* and some sort of major cataclysm in the distant past."

"The Sanguine Ones?" Kinsey asked curiously.

Nikki snorted dryly. "She upheld this blind fascination with an ancient legend. The Sanguine Ones were allegedly the first vampires here on Earth—the purest of our kind. They led their cousins out of the caves and established the birth of our civilization. Story goes, they came from the *old* world. From a place beyond this one."

"Right," I nodded.

Kinsey frowned. "There was an *old* world?"

"Depends on who you ask," Nikki added with a shrug. "Want any evidence? Then good luck finding it. I suppose there are some older scholars who believe that fairy tale."

"What would the old world have been like?"

"Full of humans, they say," Nikki smiled evilly. "Very *delicious* humans. Enough to sustain us for eons..."

"Nikki," I protested. She only grinned wider.

I carried on, ignoring her mounting bloodlust. "Lorelei Craven was a staunch believer in all of this, to the point of pure irrationality. As with *any* legend, it's merely a rather simplified explanation for a complicated topic. It provides us with the only widespread creation theory. Some among the vampire lords believe it. I do not. I prefer evidence."

"Interesting," Kinsey noted wistfully. "Can't say this is part of a balanced education, from what I experienced."

"As it shouldn't be," I replied. "None of it is true."

"Do you really think that?" She asked Nikki.

"What does it matter?"

"I'm just curious."

Nikki grinned wickedly. "Doesn't matter now. If there ever *were* a bunch of Sanguine Ones, they're *long* dead. No use in worrying about them. But if they *did* exist... I do wonder what could have killed them all? Maybe it was a war! Can you *imagine* all that bloodshed and destruction?"

"Speaking of *Sanguine Ones*—and the *vampire lords*..." Kinsey chimed in before Nikki could delve deeper into her little fantasy. "Are we going to speak with them again?"

Nikki and I shared a look.

"Do you think it's time?" She squinted an eye.

"Perhaps," I sighed. "The world's been set off balance. For nearly a year, every last hold has withstood some sort of disaster—and they're not letting up anytime soon."

I walked to the closest flower, lightly touching a brittle petal with my fingertip. Delicate and frail, the bud cracked against my skin.

"Stonehold endures an everlasting winter," I went on. "The sun has failed to return to us. Our people continue to suffer in the pitch-black frost..."

I turned back to my vassals—particularly to Nikki. "Chaos came to our world. It just wasn't how I imagined. The Council of the Eight Holds might be the least of our worries if the world plummets into magical ruin."

My sister's eyes looked forlorn.

"You realize that *we* did this."

I looked away. "I know."

Kinsey's gaze flickered back and forth between us. "Lord Elliott, what is she talking about?"

Of course I'd known.

I'd known all along.

"None of this started until Clara left," Nikki snarled. "We were dabbling in things we didn't understand. Magic *always* comes with some sort of a price to pay, and sending someone beyond the brink of our world is *insane*. That's why you made *me* do it. I was the only one crazy enough to risk it! There's a reason the old books buried below the castle are *forbidden.*"

"I don't remember you arguing," I turned on her.

"Of course I didn't," Nikki narrowed her eyes. "I was afraid that you'd throw me off the island if I defied your wishes... and, besides that, it sounded *fun.*"

Now she was grinning again.

"The human was in *constant* danger here." I took a few menacing steps towards her, putting my face in hers. "Let me remind you that the entire reason I even *considered* banishing her is because you tried to use her as a piece of living bait. She was nearly taken into the darkest reaches of Selvara Karn for a fate worse than death itself! None of us would have *ever* seen her again!"

My sister bit back angry tears. I didn't care.

"Then, to solve that, we sent her somewhere none of us will *ever* reach her again. Don't you see?" My sister stared. "You betrayed her. You used my power to betray her."

Silence fell upon us all as I glared into Nikki's eyes. She was my blood, and she needed my help—but she tested me, as did every other bloody vampire on this island.

"I was left in the medical bay," Kinsey finally spoke, carving through the anger. "I didn't realize…"

"Yes," I confirmed gravely, turning back to confront the vampire in question. "*We* cast Clara back. Ourselves."

"Don't put that on me," Nikki warned darkly.

"I don't. I bear this burden."

"Good. Because *you* gave the order."

"After *you* failed us by interfering with her."

"You allowed a traitor into the castle. You left her alone with Clara. I knew that *somebody* would come, Elliott—but I wasn't sure which viper in the grass-stalks would be one foolish enough to try. Sabine was complex. I thought *maybe* she'd change her mind. She seemed… conflicted."

I narrowed my eyes, choosing to overlook her use of that girl's name. "Nikki… It could have all been avoided."

She glowered defiantly. "Don't make laugh. *You* were the one who decided to fall in **love** with her. Your twisted heart has threatened the survival of our *entire* world now. You *dare* to blame me for this? Perhaps I should have stepped aside and let the traitor *take* what she wanted!"

Nikki froze then, waiting for me to lose my composure. The look in her eyes flashed from malice to pity and back. A part of her seemed eager to turn this into more than just a battle of words.

I sighed. "Leave my sight."

"Elliott... wait."

I turned my back on her. "I'll call when I'm ready."

Nikki didn't move for a moment.

"Okay," she finally acknowledged.

My voice hissed. "*Don't* make me repeat myself."

I felt her abandon my presence. My sister bolted away, scrambling up across the nearest castle wall in an effortless sample of her ferocious strength and agility.

"That was..." Kinsey started to speak.

"*Unnecessary*, and we will not speak of it further."

We stood quietly together for a few seconds, feeling the weight of the oppressive chill. After a moment, her curious stare burned into the back of my head. "So... what now?

I crossed my arms, debating for a moment to make up my mind. "I think that it's finally time."

Kinsey leaned on her spear. "Time for what?"

"I must convene the castle. We will discuss what comes next. We must unify the island. There are hard decisions to be made about the future of our hold... and when that is done, I must convene the Council of the Eight Holds."

She lit up.

"What?" I snapped.

"Well, that's the most reasonable thing I think that I've heard from you in a year," Kinsey smiled warmly. "Which factions should I contact?"

I looked at the frozen flowers. If this winter continued on another month or two, it was quite possible *everything* in this garden would die.

My mind was made up.

"*All of them.*"

CHAPTER 20
CLARA

A t half six in the morning, my stepfather rushed around and checked a few things. Meanwhile, I quietly rubbed the sleep from my eyes, standing in the foyer. His checked luggage—three slovenly bags—rested in a musty pile against the wall.

"Can't be too sure," I could hear him mumbling. "If there's some way to ruin this place, she'll find it..."

I didn't have the energy to argue. Had I been a little more awake, I could have probably thought of a million things I'd rather do than find some way to sabotage this decrepit old house...

Starting with sleep, I smiled to myself.

"Oi! Get that stupid grin off your face!"

I held back a sigh and let my smile fall.

Portly old Harold stumbled into the room, bumping

his luggage and nearly toppling it over. He dug around in his pockets and fished out a scrunched ball of paper, flattening it against the wall before shoving it pointedly into my hands.

"Your chore list," he declared spitefully.

I glanced down. His chicken-scratch handwriting was rough on the eyes, and he'd obviously taken great lengths to jot down anything he could think of.

"I fully expect all of that to be done by the time I get back from London," he smirked. "And don't you think of waiting until the last second. If I'm not enjoying myself down there, I'm coming back early—and I expect this *all* taken care of. No excuses."

I nodded, trying to force back a yawn.

"Oi! I'm talking to you!"

"Yes sir," I acknowledged. "It'll be done, sir."

Harold set his jaw and glowered for a moment as he searched my eyes. "Good," he finally nodded, satisfied. "Spoiled little miss, thinking you can live here rent-free without putting in the effort..."

Again, I didn't have the energy to argue.

"Help me get these to the car."

I forced what little vigor I had left in my limbs into scooping up his luggage, one massive, overweight bag at a time. Harold pushed the door open and waddled over to the boot of his car as I fought the bag over. *At least he has the decency to hold the door and pop the back...*

It took a few minutes to lurch Harold's entire set of luggage into the back of his ancient, filthy old car, but the Herculean task was eventually finished. I wiped my brow with the back of my hand as he stumbled over to the driver's side and climbed into the vehicle, swaying it with his weight.

Oh no, I realized. *What if it doesn't start?*

But then, after what were possible the longest few seconds of my life so far, Harold's car finally wheezed to life. My stepfather fidgeted with the dials for a moment before hastily rolling down his driver window to glare at me one last time.

"Don't you forget—that *whole* chore list. Everything will be done before I'm back, or you'll spend the bloody summer indoors scrubbing the floorboards!"

"Yes sir," I answered sleepily, well aware that he'd already put that one on the list.

With a grunt, Harold pulled the car out of park and shifted it onto the street. Just like that, for the first time in upwards of a year, he was out of my life again.

I was so happy that I cried.

TWO DAYS LATER, THE DOORBELL RANG. MY CHEST swelled with anxiety as I paused to gaze at myself one last time in the bathroom mirror.

I hoped that my efforts would be enough for him.

"Coming!" I shouted out towards the door.

Quickly finishing my last few little dabs of makeup, I hastily darted out towards the front door. I gave a little twirl of my black dress in the foyer mirror just to check myself out before I answered the second ring of the bell.

Peter stood in the doorway in a slimming black suit and a widening smile. "Well, look at you!"

I scrunched up my face. "Oh, stop it."

"You look fantastic," he whistled. "Own it, girl."

My eyes rolled—secretly, I adored those compliments. "Okay, so what now? Even if Harold was here, there's no way he'd do prom pictures."

"I didn't think that part was necessary," Peter smirked. "I think there's supposed some part here where I'm meant to do something with a corsage but, let's be honest... this rental alone ate up the budget."

"Yeah, you picked a good suit," I nodded approvingly. I looked behind him. "So, I'm guessing that's the car?"

My date slyly glanced over his shoulder. "You guess correctly. Mum and Dad are letting me use it tonight—so long as I don't ding the thing up."

"I didn't know you could drive," I crossed my arms.

"Of course I can drive. My folks believed in teaching me young. I've been driving since I was, like, old enough to reach the pedals. You should have seen me—when I rolled in, I aced that driver's exam with flying colours."

I smiled tenderly. "Peter, you'd have won in confidence alone. I'll bet the little old lady didn't even actually make you sit the driving portion."

"Old guy, actually," he shrugged. "I smacked him with the traditional Tatham charm, too. Dude didn't know what hit him until he was handing me my permit."

"Can't say I don't believe that." I chuckled, shaking my head. "Well, I'm sure it's a nice car and all, Peter, but I'm not sure I want to spend the night staring at it. How about we hit the road before Harold changes his mind and drives all the way back?"

He twirled the keys around his finger.

"Good call. Let's ride!"

JUST AS PETER HAD SAID, THE EVANSHIRE ACADEMY prom was taking place in a hotel downtown.

It was actually nicer than he'd thought—turns out, our school spared no expense to provide a luxurious and fun venue for our last event as their students. After this night, we had the Real World™ to look forward to—a terrifying realm made of overwhelming bills, rampant uncertainty, and our futures to inevitably mess up.

But for one last, fleeting night...

Well, we can still be kids.

Peter parked our chariot and walked over to my door,

popping it open for me like a gentleman. He helped me out with an extended elbow; I graciously took his arm.

"Why, thank you," I smiled at him.

Peter beamed. "Not at all, my dear."

The first thing that I noticed when we entered the prom was that it was, well... surprisingly *modest*. Streamers and balloons set off the décor, and there were several tables of snacks and—

"Beer!" Peter chuckled. "They've got *beer!*"

I laughed. "I guess so. I didn't think for a *second* that they'd actually *serve us* this stuff. Half this place is going to be trashed by midnight. Makes you wonder what our teachers were thinking, giving a ton of free beer at a party to freshly-legal teens..."

"I know, right? How do the Americans manage?"

"They don't," I shrugged. "*Preeeeetty* sure that drinking is illegal before twenty-one across the pond."

"Bunch of savages, them. That's no way to live."

As Peter led me towards a table near the back, I snuck a look at all of the other dresses. They looked so gorgeous. Suddenly, I felt a few self-conscious pangs over what was comparatively a conservative black dress at best.

"They're so beautiful," I murmured.

Peter smirked. "Not as much as you."

I cut him a loaded glance. "Oh, shut up."

"It's prom night," he chuckled. "Indulge me."

Unsurprisingly, it was his friends at the table. Billy and Packer were curled up together, while Sam sat to the side with a girl I didn't recognize.

"Look who finally showed," Billy grinned at us.

"Yeah, yeah..." I returned his smile. "Just be freaking glad I made it at all."

"Can't say that we're not," Sam chimed in.

"Seriously, dude," Packer smirked knowingly at Peter. "Your girl looks utterly fantastic. It's good to see you two finally getting together."

I almost choked on the spot.

"Oh, it's not like that," Peter chimed in quickly.

Packer winked. "*Riiiiight...*"

The rest of them shared a look. At this point, as far as I was concerned they could all think whatever they wanted. The embarrassment on Peter's face told me that he agreed.

"Let me go get you a drink," he chuckled.

"Sounds great. Non-alcoholic, please."

"Fair enough!"

When he disappeared over to the beverage table, I took a seat at the table with his friends.

"Virgin?" Billy chuckled.

I almost choked on the spot. "What?"

"Virgin drinks?" Packer noted knowingly, smiling all

the while. "There's an open bar out tonight, Clara! Would have thought you might really let your hair down."

I sighed and reached into my perfected imaginary self; I flashed the others a sly grin and a wink. "Oh, the night's still young! There's *plenty* of time to cut loose..."

"True that," Sam grinned with a tipsy giggle.

Billy looked like he was about to say something. That's right when Peter showed up with drinks. I happily took a cup of sprite off his hands while he kicked back half a beer.

The table cheered him on—even I got into it.

"See that? You're gonna have to play catch-up with him," Packer nudged me lightly with a smirk.

"Oh, I don't know about all *that*..."

"No?" Billy asked curiously. "Why not?"

"I don't really drink," I shrugged. "Not my thing."

"Oh." He looked a tad disappointed. "I thought that you were a bit cooler than that."

That immediately rubbed me the wrong way.

"Hey now," Peter instantly cut in, sensing discomfort. I was grateful to see him run interference on what could have suddenly become an *incredibly* awkward moment for the table. "Clara, you ready for a dance?"

If it hadn't been for Billy's annoying remark—and my persona, filling my veins with way more confidence than I should reasonably have had—I might've turned the offer down at every opportunity that night. But, very recently, I had found myself eager for a distraction—and the dance floor clearly had room for two more.

"Yeah, alright. "I took his hand. "Let's go for it."

If only I'd known what was already coming for me.

CHAPTER 21
CLARA

The night went on beautifully from there.

But it wasn't meant to last.

There have been times that have altered my life forever—things that lined up out of pure chance, only to fundamentally move me onto a path I didn't expect and could never see coming. The next of these moments came for me out of nowhere, right then and there.

It all started by incidentally turning my face.

Across the crowd, I saw the back of a brunette head. His hair was cut short; as he shifted in place, I saw how it framed a handsome and beautifully pale face.

"E-Elliott?" I gasped aloud.

The throng parted. His broad, powerful frame quickly stood out to me among the crowd—and then, as his blue, piercing eyes made contact with my own, I felt my beating heart swell in ways I thought impossible...

"Elliott?" I repeated again, louder. "Is that *you?*"

I took two tentative steps forward before his face became clearer in the throng. As the realization dawned on me, I felt all the light seep from my soul.

No. It's not him.

"Clara?" Peter asked, his hand now on my shoulder. "Wait, did you just say 'Elliott'? Wasn't that the name of the..." His body stiffened sternly beside me. "All this time, I thought you'd finally moved past those delusions. But I get it now. You're still clinging to them, aren't you?"

"Don't do this right now," I pleaded.

The look on his face crushed me.

But it was my disappointment with the misplaced face in the crowd that tugged at my heartstrings harder, utterly undoing them like a knot with a firm yank.

I felt myself unraveling where I stood.

"That was a *year* ago," Peter replied coldly. "Clutching onto these fantasies isn't healthy. You know I'll help you in any way that you need, but you've *got* to move past them. You'll never get on with your life otherwise, Clara!"

I could barely focus on his words. Running fire hit my mind, racing across my thoughts and burning them to ash in my head. My entire mental state felt like it was ripping apart at the seams, tearing into nothingness. My perfectly crafted persona slipped down into the cracks in the back of my mind, right when I needed her most...

My amulet abruptly felt heavy around my throat.

"Clara? Are you listening to me? Are you...?"

My soul felt buried beneath a terrible weight, and it pulled me down into an abyss. Part of me knew I was here, standing in an end-of-school prom—but another part knew that I was being tugged away from myself, down into a void within my body that had only grown over this horrible year. Filling this abyss was every ounce of painful grieving that I had failed to cope—and there was too much of it. It was drowning me on the inside.

The void grew darker as I fell deeper into it.

Desperate to feel the light against my skin once more, I reached up to it with clutching fingers, only to watch it fade far above me with every passing second...

"Clara?" I could hear Peter's voice in the distance. It sounded like concern, but I was just focusing on keeping myself standing upright. "Clara, are you alright?"

I wasn't falling into a pit of despair.

I was here—in a room that started to spin.

Steeling myself against the edge of a table, I was sure that other people were staring at me now; I could feel their oppressive, judging gazes on my back.

But that was the very least of my worries.

My throat could barely swallow. I felt the panic rise in my lungs like bile, threatening to choke me to death. The crushing feeling filled my windpipe and sucked out the air. *Get a grip, Clara,* I insisted inside.

The persona had completely and utterly failed me.

I was just a weak, very screwed-up girl.

*Maybe that's all I've **ever** been...*

Strong, confident hands spun me back around in place. It was my Peter, furrowing his eyebrows while he took me by the shoulders. "Wait. Clara—what's wrong?" His gaze flooded with a complicated concoction of confusion. "I'm sorry, I didn't mean to push too far—it's just that you—"

It wasn't him.

It wasn't even his words.

It was the cruel, tantalizing vision of my Elliott Craven in the crowd that ripped my soul asunder. All it had taken to completely undo me was one shining glimmer of hope; it simply made me realize that there was no going back.

I would never forget him. I'd never move past him.

This much was so painfully clear to me now that the sorrow eclipsed the last of the fleeting joy left in my heart. Whatever brief happiness that this night was supposed to bring to me... it was too late for that now.

I'd been a fool to think I could come here with my best friend, pretending beyond rationality that everything was going to be perfectly fine. The simple truth was staring me in the face, mocking me for daring to ever deny it. There was nothing more left to do than acknowledge the single foundational fact of my life: even worlds apart, my heart was forever and eternally bound to Elliott Craven.

I came to an awareness of my surroundings.

Peter's blazer hung around my shoulders; he escorted me away from the others in the crowd. But I knew that what I truly needed now, despite his love and caring, Peter Tatham sadly could not give to me. He never could.

"I…I'm sorry, Peter," I whispered to him.

"Sorry for what? Let's get you out of here."

I shook my head. "I… I can't."

He seemed perplexed. "You can't what?"

There weren't any words left to explain what happened to me—and why I just couldn't be near him anymore. I felt utterly helpless now. This was supposed to be *his* night—or, I guess *our* night.

But the ghosts of the past just wouldn't stay buried in their graves. I knew from the bottom of my heart that, no matter how badly I wanted to convince myself that it was possible… *I can never let you go, Elliott. Even if it kills me.*

"I have to leave," I replied sadly.

"Okay," Peter nodded. "Let's get you going."

I shook my head again. "I have to go alone."

"*Alone?*" He looked stunned and betrayed. "Why?"

I plucked off his blazer and shoved it into his hands. "I'm so sorry, Peter. You don't deserve this."

"Clara?" His eyes pleaded with me.

Before Peter could reply, I turned away from him— and I bolted through the confused and staring crowd, covering my mouth with a trembling hand.

I knew where I had to go.

And if it failed me *this* time, I knew that I couldn't bear to go on another single day.

CHAPTER 22

ELLIOTT

Buried deep in the Earth, *somewhere* on my world, the council chamber stood just as inhospitable and desolate as ever. Eight thrones sat in a circle, facing one another with invisible magical barriers separating them all and a gap in the center—each throne holding its back to a long passageway, leading to a secret portal and a separate castle on the world.

Each throne currently held a vampire lord.

"Greetings, Lord Craven," the ever-diplomatic Mattias Blackburn spoke as I took my own. "I believe this is the first time you have convened the council yourself."

The others watched me carefully. Their faces were a sea of emotions—all negative in some way.

"I haven't directly heard from any of you in a year."

"Is that *unusual?*" Eyes-Like-Fire snickered. A curious

and feral woman, the tribal vampire lord of the nomadic Timberland Plains licked her fangs in an open-mouthed grin. Clara called her home hold *North America*, if memory still served. *Well, what lay below Mattias Blackburn's kingdom in her world's 'Canada', at any rate...* "Before you took your throne, Lord Craven, this chamber might sit untouched for years at a time. It is only *recently* that we have had to join each other so very often..."

"Fine. I considered it time that we spoke again."

"Oh?" Ebony old Akachi Azuzi replied coldly, stroking his dangling white beard. "How considerate of you."

I ignored them both.

"The last that we met, I understand tempers flared," I replied confidently. "That was before the natural disasters overcame our world. Even as we speak, Stonehold suffers beneath a *yearlong* winter. The light has not touched my subjects in many months. I am certain all of you face your *own* troubles..."

They nodded in unison but offered nothing more.

"And I am willing to admit that I have been distrustful of you all. We did not part on the *best* of terms. But, if you meant to punish me, you've had all year to do so. I think that you've prioritized your own people's safety over any perceived sleight from Stonehold..."

Some of them smiled curiously. Others glowered.

"It's clear to me that our holds are besieged with forces beyond our control. This isn't the time for us to turn on one another. Instead of struggling while apart, what I am proposing is that we find a way to cooperate."

"Cooperate?" Valentine Vasiliev scoffed. The fearsome ruler of The Wastes scowled in open contempt—older than most of us, she oversaw the nearly inhabitable wasteland that Clara called *Russia*. "Just like how you cooperated when you had a *human* in your possession?"

I anticipated that remark. "I think that you'll find I've learned from my mistakes."

The others laughed riotously.

Meanwhile, I smiled—calm and collected.

"Oh how *wise* you've become, Lord Craven," came the melodic voice of Chanda Song, the ruler of Alevorra. Her domain was called *Southeast Asia* on Clara's world. "All it takes is half a year sulking in a tower..."

Good, I thought. *They underestimate me...*

"You did this," Svetlana Lovrić of the Drenchlands said dryly. "Sending that human away. Lord Craven, *you* called down this worldwide plague upon us."

I sighed. "We went over this all a year ago."

"Say whatever you wish to say," she shrugged aloofly. "It changes nothing. I have had a long time now to study what you've done to the fabric of our world, and the truth is very clear to me. My instruments do not lie. When you sent her back to her home-world, it expended a great deal of magic—and then, to balance that magnitude, our world has *compensated*."

"Speculation and little more," I insisted.

"The great thing with *applied science*, my Lord Craven, is that it operates independently of your beliefs. No matter what you say, my machines paint a clear picture—none of this happened until you sent her away."

I balked at that. "I did *not* send that girl *anywhere*," I lied through my fangs.

"Yes, you did. The magical disturbance originated on this world, not on the other. It is vampiric in origin. If not you, then somebody *else* in your hold banished her—and the responsibility still lays at your feet."

"What do you mean, '*vampiric in origin?*'"

Svetlana chuckled mirthlessly. "Oh, I do not think that you would want to paint me into this corner, Lord Craven. It might not exactly be to your benefit." As she smiled, she clearly **knew** something—and knowledge like that could be dangerous for *everyone* assembled here.

"I know next to nothing about your infernal machines, Lady Lovrić. Do you *seriously* expect me—or any of us—to take you at face value in your accusations?"

"Of course I do," she replied coldly. "My machines were set to study magical disturbances across the world. I will allow any vampire lord to study any readouts that my instruments produce—on what details they *can* provide, they are indisputably accurate. I know for a fact that there was a *tremendous* burst of energy the very moment that we all felt that girl leave... and, at the heart of it, a spell."

My jaw set. "There *was* no spell."

Svetlana accused with her eyes. "You lie, Lord Craven. You lie to us all. There *was* a spell—a strong and unwieldy one, leaving an unmistakable trace. Furthermore, the spell that you ordered to be cast was done by someone whose veins carry the blood of the vampire lords."

"It might have been the sister," Akachi Azuzi firmly glared at me. "She can perform magic."

"My sister is insane," I countered. "The last time she did *anything* with magic, it killed the heir to the Stonehold throne. Do not pretend I consider her a trustworthy ally."

Akachi snarled. "She's had a *hundred years* to learn how to manage it. She'd make a powerful friend with her mind in the right place... maybe a powerful *sorceress*... or maybe something lesser. Maybe a *witch*."

The others turned to me in unified indignation.

I felt this spiraling out of my control.

"I did not call this meeting to defend myself against wild, baseless accusations. My goal is to figure out how we can solve the problems of our holds. If you are unwilling to compromise or cooperate, then I'll take my leave."

EMMA GLASS

"That's not advisable," Svetlana replied coolly.

I slowly turned my head to her.

"Are you threatening me?"

"Of course not, Lord Craven." She grinned studiously. "I simply thought you'd like to hear that, just *maybe*, you can see your precious human again after all."

What I wouldn't have given to hear those words from anyone but the vampires assembled in this chamber. They sat silent, waiting to see how I would respond.

"Excuse me?" I replied in monotone.

"Since deducing how you sent her away—partly, at the very least—my next step was obviously to figure out how to bring the human back. I *planned* to save this discovery until I had some tangible results, but..." Svetlana glanced around the other thrones, clearly feeling out the room, "we have been conducting some curious experiments. I believe my scientists have pinpointed a trail leading away from this world. There might be a way to contact the humans—but it hinges on bringing that girl back. She is key."

Her eyes finally focused on mine.

"Wouldn't that be *grand?*"

No, I gasped in my mind. *This can't be.*

"Well!" Akachi laughed, turning to me. "What good news! You must be *overjoyed* to hear that—you sounded so *finished* with her last time, but you know what they say... '*Absence makes the heart grow fonder!*'" He wiped a dark tear from his eye. "Either way, I think you'll find that I—and all the others—will still hold you to your old promise..."

The mirth faded from his face as he lowered angry eyes upon me. "If that human steps foot upon this world again, you *promised* to hand her over to us. I think, Lord Craven, that you will find our patience is *already* at its limit..."

Mattias spoke now, turning to Svetlana. "This is quite the turn of events, Lady Lovrić. Tell me, how soon could this be accomplished?"

"Not soon," she sighed drearily. "We suffered setbacks. Earlier this year, we endured a magical rupture that laid waste to the primary engine. It took us two months to rebuild it back to specifications—and I'm not in any hurry for history to repeat so dramatically..."

"I remember feeling that disturbance," I mentioned.

"Yes," Eyes-Like-Fire agreed. "Me too."

The others nodded as well.

"It *feels* like a leap beyond this world because, in a way, it *is* one," Svetlana continued. "The calibrations aren't easy to master. It will take me months further to finish them, maybe a year..." Her gaze slid my way with a mocking smirk. "Then again, I received such bountiful, *excellent* raw data from her last time crossing the worlds... I expect that it wouldn't take long to tweak the algorithms. With luck, we may draw her back by year's end."

"How does it work?" I asked furiously.

"We've discovered an echo—like a trail. The human left it in her wake. My best scientists have been steadily amplifying it for the past half a year, trying to coordinate a pinpoint that exists *outside* our ethereal boundaries. Once we've determined her position, we can pull her back."

"Even without knowing what hides on the other side?" Mattias noted calmly. "Is that *wise?*"

"This does sound dangerous," I responded coldly.

"I recall some saying the same thing about chrysm ore when its utilitarian purposes were discovered," Svetlana replied sternly. "And yet, I also recall that none stood in the way of progress then. Why should we do so now?"

"Forging contact with a world of humans," Akachi stroked his white beard again. "What a peculiar thought. If that girl had never come, we may have never discovered *any* of this!" My nemesis turned to me, his expression the very face of triumphant malevolence. "Lord Craven, be a sport and *do* remind me to thank her when I see her next... it sounds like it won't be long."

I rose up from my seat.

"I can see now that this was fruitless."

"Lord Craven," Mattias stopped me. "There is much to discuss on this topic. We have not adjourned—and I am imploring you to retake your seat."

I let my gaze drift among the vampire lords.

Each one dwelled on the endless possibilities of us all reaching out to the human world—a world for the taking, filled with legendarily alluring blood. The thought of these thirsty vampires gaining access to a tantalizing realm filled me with equal parts terror and fury.

"No," I replied darkly.

He was clearly taken aback. "Are you relinquishing your place at this discussion, Lord Craven?"

I turned my back and left their company.

And, like long ago, I let my silence serve as my reply.

When I returned to my throne room, Nikki and Kinsey stood in wait.

"Brother," Nikki started. "I wanted to say that—"

"It doesn't matter," I replied bitterly.

"Oh." Her eyes darkened. "Great. Good to know."

"No," I sighed, taking my seat back within the throne. "That's not what I meant. I am not looking for apologies, Nikki. I've got much bigger concerns to deal with."

My sister's eyes flickered thoughtfully.

Kinsey tilted her head inquisitively. "Suppose it's safe to say that the Council didn't go over so well?"

"No," I replied in mounting anger.

Nikki lowered to a knee beside me, her eyes filled with a surprising empathy. "Elliott... what did they do?"

My chest felt tighter than ever before. The entire room was spinning now, and nothing I did would make it stop. *This is all a nightmare,* I thought in rising, despondent rage. *Just one long, waking nightmare...*

"The Drenchlands have been... *active*."

Nikki's face fell. "Oh no."

"Oh yes," I replied bleakly. "Our dear friend under the sea, Svetlana Lovrić, has been busily searching for a way to bring Clara back to our world—into *her* hold this time. She thinks she can establish a way to contact her world."

"How is that possible?" Kinsey asked.

"I don't know. The explanation was far beyond me. But whatever she has created, I believe her story." I turned to my sister again. "They know it was us who cast Clara out. She knew things—and told them that somebody with the blood of a vampire lord cast the spell..."

"Did they mention me?"

I sighed. "They did. Well, Akachi did."

The atmosphere in the throne room darkened further. All three of us stared into space for a few minutes, none willing to ask the obvious question. It was Nikki who did.

"They're finally going to attack us, aren't they?"

"Yes," I nodded. "They will come soon."

"How can we prepare?" Kinsey asked despairingly.

I sighed heavily. "The first step will be to assemble the factions of the castle. I'll need to take better stock of our defenses and prepare the island for war. It's likely that the vampire lords will attack the main stronghold, and we can use that to our advantage..."

I paused, sensing something dividing my attention.

"Elliott?" Nikki lifted a brow.

"The main... stronghold..." I repeated, feeling oddly drawn away from my thoughts. "They'll attack..."

"Lord Elliott?" Kinsey asked. "Are you alright?"

I suddenly couldn't concentrate. My attention blown to the winds, I simply couldn't put my finger on it. Whatever the catalyst... I *felt* it before I saw it happen. My words utterly failed me now—but I knew *something* formidable was nearby. It eluded definition.

I hissed to my side. "Do you feel that?"

"Feel what?" Kinsey asked devotedly.

"Something's coming," I snarled, glancing around now in a frenzied panic. "Whatever it is, it's strong. It's here, in the castle... it's right..."

My eyes settled halfway down my throne room.

"Right... there..."

Nikki suddenly gasped. "Holy..."

"You can feel it too?" My eyes snapped to her.

She looked thrilled. "It's... *powerful*..."

I clenched my armrests. "And it's coming!"

In an instant, a colourful, magical tempest whipped up into life before my very eyes, sending a startled hysteria throughout my royal guards. It was incredible to witness it fizzle into existence in front of me—it carved out a wide bubble of overwhelming majesty.

I could barely grasp what I was seeing.

"What *is* that?" Kinsey gasped.

Nikki merely smiled. She knew before I did.

With the blink of an eye, I realized that I could sense the emotions of every vampire in the room—and after that discovery, I became distinctly and acutely aware of every last speck of dust...

Ten minutes after I fled, I stepped onto a bus.

It was mostly deserted, luckily. I dropped my coins into the till as I stepped on and picked a seat near the back, where I knew I'd be alone. As I brushed past them, a few stray pairs of eyes lifted to follow me for a few seconds. Nobody seemed interested in me; their attention, it seemed, quickly evaporated from me.

After I settled down into the seat, I rested my forehead against the window. My heart was heavier now than I'd ever known before.

Eager for a distraction, I focused instead on how I felt the bus lurching beneath me. It ambled around a corner and pulled over to another stop up the line.

I felt so painfully empty inside.

Time passed. Others came on or left the bus. There were never more than a few lost souls here, just like me.

I wondered what drove them all.

A beanie-headed girl near me sat with earbuds in, bobbing her head to the beat of her music. I could barely hear the slightest, almost inaudible static of the song. She looked cool—I wondered, in another life, if perhaps we could maybe have been friends.

An old man sat facing into the aisle. His frail body rocked with every bounce of the bus; his face was frozen in a look of contemplation, or maybe sadness.

There were others.

A university student texted up a storm on his phone; a woman sat with a large paper bag of groceries under one arm; a young, attractive couple quietly rested together.

The zoned-out looks on all their faces reminded me of my old friends, the Knightly Trio.

I turned away, unable to cope with that.

I finally let myself feel the feeling that I'd avoided all day and all night. A mounting pressure inside grew desperate for release, but I couldn't bring myself to cry.

What I did instead was whisper a name.

Elliott.

I craved his touch once again.

Those piercing blue eyes smirked at me, deep in my memories. I longed for that pale, handsome skin and the way he cupped my cheek as he matched my loving gaze. For most of our time together, I lived in constant danger from the other vampires of his castle. He found himself resisting the allure of my human blood, struggling to keep me at arm's length all the while. I didn't know what to do about my developing feelings for him—and our growing attraction for each other.

It became increasingly clear to me that he *truly* cared. Even the ridiculous lengths that he went to to celebrate my seventeenth birthday showed me the elusive vampire lord wanted me to be happy. Then there came the pain of our swift separation, when he watched me get flung back out from his world... *I didn't understand how brief our time was. If I ever get to see you,* I promised myself and him, *I'll **never** take our time together for granted again.*

And thus, on a dark night in a quiet English town, I stared out a bus window and let my thoughts dwell on my beloved, a vampire named Elliott.

IT WAS ONLY NATURAL TO GET OFF AT THE VILLAGE.

Under the blackened night, the rain sprinkled down. Any other evening, I'd have reconsidered or darted away for cover, eager to get out from even the slightest rainfall.

But tonight? Tonight, I walked in a daze.

My footsteps were drawn now by something bigger than me—Grief? Remorse? Regret? I couldn't tell. It didn't even really matter to me anymore.

The wet streets glistened from the streetlights. The few wandering townsfolk walked along the pavement under their umbrellas or newspapers, and nobody paid me any mind. I passed a few restaurants and considered jumping in and ordering something warm and dry, but I couldn't bring my feet to stop.

Along the way, I spotted a familiar alley.

Sure enough, the rusted sign for old Broadmoor Park barely hung at the end, dangling against the gate. Strides took me right up to it—I crouched in front, brushing my fingertips along the raised lettering. "I'm really sorry that I haven't been to see you in a while," I told it quietly, frowning with tears in my eyes. "Maybe I should have. I hope you know I've missed you."

I felt like the sign understood.

It seemed appropriate that the ribbon was still here, even if it was soiled and dingy from the elements. *Thank you for holding it together for me.* I resisted the urge to brush a fingertip against it, afraid that it might finally give out at my touch.

The rain was starting to pick up a little. I rose up from my crouch and pushed around the half-open gate, wanting to get beneath the cover of the tree canopy.

It was darker than I remembered in here—then again, I'd never been here after twilight. I pulled out my phone and turned on the flashlight, brightening up the winding path forward for myself. Walking the broken trail felt like going through the motions again, aimlessly chasing after some distant place I knew that I'd never reach.

Or maybe it felt like coming home.

As I wandered, so did my mind. There was nothing left to keep me here. Harold made it painfully clear that I wasn't welcome in his house as anything greater than a slave; secondary school was over, and my path ahead remained unclear; Peter, oh my precious Peter, as much as I hated to admit it—he could never stand to fill the void in my heart left by the one I truly loved.

I dwelled on that: *there is nothing left here for me.*

In the dark, the trees reminded me of the forest from my nightmares. But I knew that there was no force of malevolent nature here that wanted to destroy me. The only enemy I had here came from within—the grief that opened in my heart like a deep and endless well, choking every last little drop of joy from my soul.

It wasn't like I had much of that left, anyway.

The edge of the trees came into view. I pushed out into the night, mildly aware that the sprinkling rain had chosen to take pity on me. The air hung heavy and the grass dripped with water as I followed the broken path of the pavement along the edge of the lake that changed my life.

There was the dock.

There was nothing else.

But something told me that I had to be there now. I felt this rise from inside like a whisper, lost in the night and too quiet to catch on the wind.

The impulse was not a healthy one, but I obeyed.

Planks creaked as I stepped onto the slickened wood. I carefully climbed up the stairs and began walking over the wet, protesting boards, not sure what I possibly hoped I could accomplish where I'd failed countless times before. My mind slowly emptied until I stood at the edge of the platform. I stared thoughtlessly into the blackened abyss of the dark lake, unable to go any further.

Depression is a creature of meticulous patience. Once it has you in its grasp, it grinds down your spirit beneath its oppressive weight. Then, once you finally begin cracking underneath the unbearable pressure, it starts to hollow you out from the inside—one painstaking bite at a time.

I truly thought I understood depression before. But the feelings I felt while dealing with Harold, even at his best? They were *nothing* like this. What I felt now was pure grief at the hardest that I'd ever known it. It sunk down into my every bone inside my body. Try as I might, there was no stopping the realization as it struck me in the face.

This life isn't enough.

A flood of emotion cascaded the entirety of my soul. I felt the crashing waters of utter misery force down my screaming mind down into the deepest, darkest depths it had ever felt. My spirit gasped for air, drowning in sorrow. The water was so strong in my soul that it burst out of me, rolling down my face in salty tears so powerful that my whole body shuddered.

The grief threatened to swallow me alive.

I can't do this, I gasped.

I can't go back to this...

As I trembled with sobs that racked my shoulders, my eyes began to sting. I wiped away at them with the back of my wrist, but the pain only worsened.

I opened my eyes, and I gasped.

The amulet around my neck pulsed now with a dark but vibrant sheen. The colours reminded me of a distant sky that I could only see in my dreams—in a purple base, the amulet glowed green, then blue, then pink, then red, all in waves that blended seamlessly into one another, each fighting for a turn. This wasn't just *inside* the amulet at my neck, either. As the colours began dancing in the air before me, the brightening light bathing a pale, bluish hue...

The pulsations pounded like a heartbeat on my skin. *No, wait... that **is** my heartbeat!*

Flashes of long-lost memory struck me.

For the first time in a year, I remembered what it was like to tumble through countless galaxies and exploding dimensions in that abyss—*just like what happens when I leave behind another world*, I realized.

And then—like that—the amulet burst into life.

Everything around ripped apart into a swirling vortex. The abandoned park and its lake exploded away into a comforting abyss, far less violent than the utter insanity I'd felt before. Soothing colours of teal and blue whirled around me in a watery, dreamlike state; I held my arms up to buffet the roaring wind.

That's right, I thought as defiantly as I could.

TAKE ME TO ELLIOTT.

The wind raged as the colours faded into a pinkish and teal glow. The surrounding otherworldly abyss was still too sharp for me to directly see—at times, I had to clamp shut my eyes to protect them.

But this time, traveling was different. *Much* different.

It wasn't just the subtle changes in my scenery. Instead of plummeting through a violent chaos, I realized I stood on my own two feet still. A solid surface stretched beneath me like white sand; I watched as the particles frayed away from the edges, rising up into the soothing chaos.

From behind my shielding forearm held up high in front, I could barely make out something else behind the veil. The watery void gave way to darkened details—a magnificent hall I had seen many times with my lost love.

The abyss dissolved down around me.

Across the throne room on a world I never thought I'd ever see again, I gazed into the startled and piercing eyes of the man I thought I'd never see again.

"Elliott," I whispered, overcome with emotion.

In a heartbeat, he stood up from his chair. I could see others were assembled with him—Nikki stood at his side, and there was a young female royal guard next to him that I didn't recognize. I couldn't see any of my Knightly Trio standing guard—Wilhelm, Viktor, and Asarra—but I did see recognizable others along the edges of the room.

"Clara..." Elliott gasped, transfixed. "How did you..."

I felt a quick pulse of power from the Blackwell Amulet like a convulsion, radiating across my body. As I cried out in surprise, the magical throb bent me over, forcing me to hold tightly onto my own shoulders. My eyes clamped shut with pain; the moment passed just as I felt a strong, powerful presence throw its arms around me.

"E-Elliott?" I looked up into his surprised stare.

Before he could answer, I realized that something felt

intensely wrong. My instincts kicked in *hard*, and they told me that I needed to pull from him—and *right now*.

"Wait—Elliott, get away from me, before—"

But it was too late.

The otherworldly abyss roared back to life around me, swallowing away the throne room again. Swirling blue and pinkish tones whirled outside the small sandbar as the tenacious winds burst back onto the scene.

There was just enough room for the two of us.

...***Two*** *of us?!*

I blinked up at Elliott. Instinctively, the vampire lord shielded me from the winds with his cloak. Neither of us could speak—the air felt ripped from our lungs as we took solace from the otherworldly gale.

I tried to warn him.

I tried to tell him to let go.

I couldn't suck in enough air to form the words. A part of me already knew that we were beyond the point of no return—and I didn't want to find what might happen if I let him go now. Unbelievably powerful magic rippled in the air around us, oblivious to our desires... and maybe oblivious to us at all.

Elliott looked me in the eyes, his face filled with fear.

We clung together as the amulet dragged us away, back onto a dilapidated dock over an abandoned lake...

EPILOGUE
LORELEI

I set out once again under the chilly moonlight.

Asleep near my tent was my mount—a relatively temperamental beast of silver fur and vicious claws. Perfectly adapted to this frozen environment, the beast kept away the predators that I could otherwise face within these foreign lands. The magic that I'd performed on the rugged monster kept it under my control.

Even if only by the barest amount.

Once I packed up my campsite, obliterating any traces of my presence, we rode hard for several hours of waning light through the wilderness. I was quite careful to keep us away from the forested areas, lest the old legends of the haunted woods prove true even here.

Instead, I took my chances with the open terrain. I was finally less than a day's ride from my destination; a few more hours, and I would arrive.

After some time, the creature and I finally came to the edge of a tall plateau of ice and snow. There, in the distance on the edge of a frozen ridge, sat the sprawling manor that I had come all this way to find.

And so we rode the final hour to reach it.

Two tall, stocky vampires clad in leather and warm furs quietly stood guard at the imposing gate. They took amused interest in me as I slipped down from the mount under the failing moonlight; my warm cloak buffeted me against the wind.

"Halt," one ordered. "Who goes there?"

"I have come to see your master."

The other chuckled. "And who are you?"

I pulled back my hood, spilling my thick, long hair out into the harsh winds. "Lorelei Craven," I answered with a glare. "Tell me my name means something, even *here* on the edge of the world."

Once they composed themselves, one guard hastily vanished through the security door. The other stood to watch over me. When we were alone, he started to pull off the thickest layer of his furs.

"What are you doing?" I raised an eyebrow.

"You did not arrive through the portal network," he noted with certainty, jabbing his thumb at the gate behind himself as he continued stripping off the fur. "Otherwise, you'd have come in from the *other* side of that door. You've had quite a long journey across the ocean and through the tundra. My Lady, you must be freezing cold."

"Your kindness is noted," I responded with no small amusement. "But I've been here in these frigid lands for a long time now. A few more minutes won't kill me."

Sheepishly, he threw the fur back over his shoulder.

A few draining minutes later, the first guard returned. His voice was cordial. "Welcome, Lady Craven. Obviously, you've been cleared to enter..." He quickly rapped out a pattern on the gate with his knuckles. Gargantuan, heavy doors slowly creaked apart. "The escort waiting inside will take you further."

"My thanks," I obligatorily replied.

Before continuing, I turned back and placed my palm on the beast. Reaching for a pocket, I grasped at a talisman and spoke a few careful words. The feral creature that had loyally carried me hundreds of kilometers to this place quickly shook its head, snarled, and stalked off away. I watched instinct return as the creature wandered into the cold tundra.

I felt nothing as we parted ways.

"Thanks for not leaving us to deal with that *thing*," the guard who had offered me furs spoke with a grin.

I ignored him.

The gate closed at my back as I crossed the threshold. Standing alone and ahead in the warm manor foyer, the steward politely offered me a reverent nod. "Lady Craven. It's been a while. Please, come this way."

As expected, the steward took me straight towards the throne room. After such a long and arduous journey, it pleased me to see this kind of courtesy and respect. With the company that I sought now, I expected a decent wait of an hour, perhaps longer. Thankfully, it seemed I could skip straight to meeting with my host.

We marched through the main hall and straight to the seat of the vampire lord. Giving a deferential bow to his master, the steward announced me.

"Presenting her royal highness, Lady Lorelei Craven."

"Thank you, Wren." The vampire lord waved him aside as he rose up from his throne. *Tall, broad, and just as brooding as I remember...* Wren was right. It had been quite some time since I had encountered Lord Mattias Blackburn without some sort of magical barrier between us.

He took one look at me and shook his head.

"Lorelei, you recall that there are more *convenient* ways of reaching me," Mattias noted dryly. "Scenic as it is, you did not have to take the long way to Bleakwood."

"It was either return to Stonehold Castle, or this," I replied with faint annoyance. "It was better this way, no matter the time I lost. The seers made it clear what will happen the next time I step foot on the Isle of Obsidian."

Mattias watched with his calm, surmising eyes. "Walk with me, Lorelei."

"I have done quite a *lot* of walking."

"Fine." He ignored that. "After such a long journey, is it right for me to assume that you'll want to rest here in the castle—as a formal guest?"

"A few days would be an appreciated gift."

He turned to his steward. "See that it is done."

The steward nodded graciously and left us, leaving only Mattias and myself—well, besides his small group of royal guards.

"Perhaps we should speak in private," he observed.

"Perhaps," I agreed apathetically.

Deep in his private royal suite, Mattias and I showered together. Afterwards, we made love in the same bed we'd shared so many nights in our long lives kept apart.

As my head lay against the beating heart of his barrel chest, he distantly played with my long hair. It was always a comfortable place to be, in his strong arms, as fleeting as our times together were. Never could we have ever been anything more than this—the union of vampire lords was *strictly* taboo. Our love was a forbidden one.

"Why have you come here, Lorelei?" He asked.

I ignored the question. "How has Elliott managed?"

"I saw him a few days ago. He convened the Council of the Eight Holds. It did not go his way, and he seemed to be quite rattled."

"Tell me more," I insisted. "Speak of the past year."

He paused. "Do you care to know?"

"Would I waste my time asking?"

Mattias sucked in a sharp inhale of air. "The vampire lords have endured their own major setbacks, but it seems your replacement has had to contend with a *powerfully* dark and menacing winter."

"I am aware," I reminded him. "I spent plenty of time on the mainland, after all. Tell me what I do not know."

My lover hesitated. "The toll this last year has taken on him has been a poorly held secret. Elliott took the human's vanishing act *quite* hard. From what I have gathered, he disappeared into your old tower in powerful grief, unseen for months at a time."

"Unfortunate. What of his reign?"

Mattias set his jaw. "A reign by decree. *Tyrannical*."

"That is... unexpected."

"True, the boy was always quite cold and calculating. Yet it seems that he has been twisted into a shadow of his former self. He rules logically, there is no denying that, but clearly a part of him was damaged in the time he shared the company of the human girl. His decisions seem to be brutally efficient, but I can see that they are shortsighted. I do not know what the others make of this —and I keep my theories close to my chest—but it is clear to me that Elliott loved the girl... and now he suffers."

Had I heard this a few years before, I might have burst into tears. Once, I had known sensations like that. Instead, I didn't feel a thing. My lover noticed this, leaning his chin down to study the top of my head.

"The curse is worsening, isn't it?"

I felt nothing at his concern, either.

"My emotions are almost entirely gone now, yes. I find it increasingly difficult to feign any of them for the sake of normalcy. To be truthful, I have nearly forgotten what they ever felt like in the first place."

Silence fell on the room as he contemplated this.

Mattias eventually asked: "Do you still love me?"

I lifted my face with a slight annoyance. "My darling, desperation doesn't suit you. My love for you is nearly all that I have left now."

"*Lying* doesn't suit you, either."

I sighed. "Call me fond, then."

Mattias turned away—his lumbering form filled with some sort of obvious disappointment.

"I *warned* you about this, Lorelei," he snarled coldly. "Dabbling in all the things that you have, all the mystical arts you've been chasing down, century after century—I *told* you that it would end like this. The curse robs you of your mind, one tiny sliver at a time. I watch *everything* that ever made me fall in love with you wither and die."

"It was necessary, Mattias. I learned that which I had to know—the truth about our realm the truth, the truth about the Sanguine Ones, the horrors of the Cataclysm. I learned everything..." I looked up at his stern eyes, forcing out a smile. "It's all true, Mattias. It *always* was."

He looked hurt and unconvinced. "Even so—how do you hope to prove such things? There isn't anyone who will believe your mad claims, especially on the council."

"They don't need to," I replied calmly.

"I don't follow."

"Their opinions will matter little with what is coming. Soon, all we have worked so fervently to accomplish will be unraveled." I lifted up my hard stare to his own again. "The black wind howls."

"The black wind is a fable," he replied coolly.

"So are humans. So are the Sanguine Ones. So is the existence of worlds beyond our own. And yet, Mattias, all of our fables are slowly drawing back to life. As spoken by my seers, and my gypsies, and my druids, and by looking through the Pierced Veil with my *own* two eyes, it all rests on the shoulders of my successor."

"Elliott," he sighed wearily.

"I know you have very little faith in him. But he is not as foolish as you think. He inherited a destiny he was never meant to carry upon his shoulders. You cannot fault him for not being prepared. For not being ready."

"That's right," Mattias shook his head despondently. "There was supposed to be *another*..."

"Fiona," I nodded quietly. "But her fate changed."

"Do you miss her?"

"I think that I used to."

"My gods, Lorelei. What's become of you?"

I didn't understand the question. Perhaps I *couldn't*.

"My love, I am merely who I am meant to be. Just as Fiona was meant to be, before what happened to her fate. Without my eldest daughter to guide the path forward, it falls to the next—to Elliott. He has become the key now."

"And the human?"

"It could have been *any* human. Pushing Fiona out of the way changed the fates. Perhaps it would have been a different human that crossed through. There's no telling. It is beyond my power to understand those things."

Before he could reply, the door knocked.

"Leave," he ordered our unwanted guest.

The knocking came again.

"That sounds insistent," I observed.

Mattias rose angrily, tossing on a robe around his body. As I slipped down beneath the covers to preserve a small measure of my dignity, my lover marched across the regal suite to answer the door.

"This had *better* be good, Wren."

There was hushed chatter. Mattias glanced back over his shoulder at me for a second, then stepped out to speak with his private steward.

It was over a minute before he came back into the

room—and when he returned, he sat on the edge of the bed and stared pensively into space.

I sat up. "What is it, Mattias?"

He did not answer immediately. "Do you remember that brief, powerful burst of magic from yesterday? I know that you felt it too. We *all* felt it."

"Yes," I nodded. "I thought that it was a turning point in the disasters striking our world, perhaps."

"And *I* thought it was Svetlana's experiments."

"I take it that we were both wrong."

He nodded. "It was something far worse."

"Was it... another human?"

"No," he shook his head.

"I do not possess much patience for guessing games," I replied coolly.

His haunted eyes turned to me. "Elliott. He is gone."

My head tilted. "Gone? How is he *gone?*"

Confused and shaken, Mattias hardened his gaze. "The human came back for him, Lorelei. That boy is no longer a part of our world. He has been taken away."

I thought on that momentarily. "If that is true, events are moving faster than I thought..."

Mattias stared blankly at me.

I caught the slightest whiff of horror in his eyes.

"Tell me then, Lorelei, in your infinite wisdom—what happens next? How do we prepare?"

"Elliott and Clara will return," I replied. "And *soon.*"

"And when he does?"

"We must hold this world together for them, Mattias," I replied, lost in reflection. "And when our *son* returns to us, everything that we've worked so hard to protect will face its day of reckoning. Something comes for us all."

"What is it?" He asked. "What is coming?"

I turned back to him. "Calamity..."

ARE YOU READY TO FIND OUT WHAT HAPPENS NEXT in Clara and Elliot's story?

A WITCH BETWEEN WORLDS #4: THE WITCH'S Dilemma is available NOW! Find it at Amazon today!

A Witch Between Worlds Series
Season #1 (Books #1-#10 is complete!)

Here's the reading order:

The Vampire's Witch (Book 1)
Trials of the Vampire (Book 2) Available Now
A Witch's Reunion (Book 3) Available Now
The Witch's Dilemma (Book 4) Available Now
The Witch's Peril (Book 5) Available Now
The Witch's Path (Book 6) Available Now
The Witch's Kiss (Book 7) Available Now
The Witch's Heart (Book 8) Available Now

The Witch's Sorrow (Book 9) Available Now
The Witch's Destiny (Book 10) Available Now!

**Look for Season 2 of A Witch Between Worlds
starting February 2019!**

The Witch's Wolf (Book 11) Available February 2019

APPENDIX

A Witch Between Worlds involves a vampire world very similar to our own, but with different names for many of the places, and certain striking differences. Some of my darling readers have asked that I add some sort of glossary for easy reference.

The following pages offer various details that may help you distinguish the distant regions and rulers of Elliott's realm—along with *trivia not yet touched upon*.

I hope it all makes for a compelling read!

-Emma Glass

HOLDS

Elliott Craven's world does not have kings, and thus any kingdoms or republics. Instead, it is divided into eight **holds**, which serve the same basic purpose.

In earlier times, there were more holds than the eight —but civil war and conquest has obliterated some of these places from the history books, and their history is sadly lost to time.

Each hold features an ancient vampire civilization of great power, separated by vast distances and untamed wilderness for all of history. Thanks to the discovery of *chrysm*, the distances between the holds have been rendered irrelevant, and the past two centuries have brought much progress in uniting the world of Vampires.

Stonehold, or *Europe,* is where our story has largely taken place so far. Characterized by its trades, all walks of labourers toil away on the mainland—from black-smiths to wood-workers to miners. Until the past few centuries, it was a relatively poor but proud worker economy. To the distant southeastern corner lay the **Far Reaches,** known for untamed wilderness and mystical gypsy tribes.

The civilization is now experiencing the tail end of a renaissance period, thanks to the revolutionary discovery of a powerful ore called *chrysm*, located here in abundance; the **Dawning Mines** in the southern **Alpine Ridge** are of particular wealth, carefully hidden from the world.

The seat of power is **Stonehold Castle** on the distant **Isle of Obsidian**, filled with vicious forests and countryside; you may know it as the *United Kingdom.* The sudden abdication of the throne by the beloved vampire lord Lorelei Craven has caused a crisis around her young and inexperienced heir, Elliott.

The Falvian Badlands, or *Africa,* is a wild land divided into three major regions. The northern third is a largely inhospitable desert; the center is a dangerous jungle; the bottom third is a foreboding swamp. Along the eastern edge runs a stark and dangerous mountain range, filled with volcanoes and chaotic lightning storms. Such a threatening environment has hardened the vampires into a vicious, self-serving people—the land is rife with thieves, bandits, outlaws, and all manner of renegades.

As the Middle East exists in another form in this world, the **Gold Coast**—what would be our world's *Cairo*—rests on the shoreline as the merchant capital of the world. Of the rampant voodoo far south, the major landmark is ***Slough's Descent***, a mystical swamp settlement near a massive canyon of tumbling bog and glowing silt (it is known to us as our largest waterfall, *Victoria Falls*).

The main castle, the foreboding **Tower of Scorch** of the **Killing Peaks**, rests atop the most active volcano of both worlds, *Mount Nyamuragira*. The intense lava flow here is restrained by ancient magic, used as a power source.

The Drenchlands, or *the Middle East,* is an archipelago of resource-stripped islands above a shallow sea. Stories tell of a time that the land was fertile and rich—but that a broken accord with nature resulted in a powerful flood that trapped the vampires on these newly formed arid islands.

Eons of overpopulation and poverty resulted in a society that encouraged intelligence and shrewdness to solve their many problems. Vampiric geniuses—with lifespans far less limited by death—have dedicated their years to the advancement of science, culminating in discoveries that have allowed their society to settle beneath the waves.

Little is known of the vampires of the Drenchlands since disappearing below the surface—only that they hold the most powerful technologies in the world. Their castle is the **Sunken Citadel**, built near the place where our world's Babylon sat.

Timberland Plains, or *America/Mexico,* is a widespread tribal land filled with every geographical option under the sun. Rolling hills, soaring mountain ranges, vast plains, parched deserts, and icy valleys fill this region.

Settlements are few and far between—the nomadic vampires of the Timberland Plains chase the hunt and move with the herds of powerful magical creatures. As a result of their respectful bond with nature, in no small part due to powerful rituals and tributes to the stars, the wildlife works in conjunction with these vampire tribes and does not lash out at them like in other holds.

Of the few permanent settlements is the castle in the desert, the **Twilight Gate**—an imposing clay fortress atop a massive sandstone bluff, built as a sacred tribute to nature. It was known in our world as *Acoma Pueblo* of present-day New Mexico, or the *Sky City*.

Bleakwood, or *Canada,* is a frigid northern landmass of hunters, trappers, and miners. The endless sea of forest complicates the profession—it is haunted to the point of open hostility with all manners of wraiths, ghouls, and banshees. Furthermore, the natural wildlife is among some of the most cunning in the realm.

Vampires here seek what little warmth they can find in cavernous settlements of the western mountain ranges, such as the subterranean **Cavern's Solace**. The greatest among these people are explorers, carving their legacies out in the frozen and threatening woods—but even they dare only to explore along the edges.

The hold is ruled from **Blackburn Manor**, owned across the ages by the eponymous family. It sits on the edge of a permanently frozen lake, what we call *Lake Louise*.

❦

Selvara Karn, or *South America,* has been overwhelmed by their world's equivalent of the *Amazon Rainforest.* Within the tropical forests breed limitless predators and swarms, empowered by unopposed magic. This greatly mystical hold, in fact, is widespread considered to be the most openly antagonistic one in the entire world. Very few to step foot there are ever heard from again.

The surviving vampires hole up in large settlements; the shamans and witch doctors of Selvara Karn harness the powerful magic that makes their lives so dangerous. It is thought that the potency of magic here is unrivaled.

World's Pillar, a towering tree akin to *Yggdrasil* of Norse mythology in the heart of *Amazonia*, serves as the major settlement and the fortified home of the vampire lord. The tree itself rises far above the forests; the shamanic colony exists as a treetop paradise, built upon the lesser trees that spout above its greatly magical roots.

❦

Alevorra, or *Southern Asia,* is a tropical paradise. Unlike Selvara Karn's rainforest gone wildly amok, Alevorra is filled instead with docile grasslands, secluded valleys, and gentle rainforests. The region enjoys diverse magical wildlife and a certain level of peace not typically seen on this world—however, a natural balance is retained with the presence of strong magical monsoons.

This region is dotted with weathered temple ruins from a time long forgotten, forming most of the settlements. One such is **Lights Fall**, half-destroyed and falling apart, called *Bagan* in what we consider *Myanmar* or *Burma*.

Another easy Selvara Karn comparison is that the castle itself is the largest settlement. Our world's *Angkor Wat* of the fallen *Khmer Empire* lives on deep in the jungles as **Sunstone Temple**. Despite nature's attempts to reclaim the tempel, the widespread city center enjoys prosperity, sustaining itself with nearby agriculture and farming.

⚜

The Wastes, or *Russia and surrounding territories,* enjoys secrecy to a degree rivaling even the Drenchlands. Little is known of the hold, with only its geography—a dark, frozen scar of tundra and mountains ripped across the world—being well recorded.

Menacing and chaotic, the Wastes are considered a glum and inhospitable wasteland that forces its citizens into safety below the world, a lifestyle further complicated by the many, *many* active volcanoes that blight the horizon. It is said that the ash in the clouds above The Wastes forever blots out the sun and the stars.

The only known place of refuge within the Wastes is the **Nether Pit,** a subterranean castle of unknown origin.

VAMPIRE LORDS

The **vampire lords** are the fearsome monarchs of their world, each ruling a separate hold. The bloodlines of the vampire lords are energized with a powerful magic that, for better or worse, strengthens their innate abilities far beyond common vampires.

Together, they form the **Council of the Eight Holds**. It is from a hidden neutral zone, bound by restrictive magic, that they make decisions that affect the entire world.

It is through a powerful ritual called the **Ascension** that a vampire lord unlocks his or her untapped potential. If a lord is toppled and the bloodline wiped out, the hold as it is known is annexed by its conqueror, and the world's magic steadily takes care of the rest.

Elliott Craven of **Stonehold** is the newest and youngest vampire lord in the world. After his beloved predecessor Lorelei Craven suddenly abdicates the throne, her son is thrust vastly unprepared onto the world stage.

Cold, calculating, and greatly concerned with protecting his people, it is increasingly clear that his love for Clara Blackwell has radically changed his path.

His castle is **Stonehold Castle** on the **Isle of Obsidian.**

❦

Akachi Azuzi of the **Falvian Badlands** is eldest among the vampire lords. Ruling over a hold known for nearly constant chaos, warfare, and greed, Akachi has survived countless mutinies against his life for the throne.

A weathered, gnarled ebony vampire with a trickster's smile knows that he grows ever older, and seeks greater power to secure his grip over his anarchic realm.

His castle is the **Scorched Tower** of the **Killing Peaks.**

❦

Svetlana Lovrić of **The Drenchlands** respects only

two things in this world: curiosity and ingenuity. Famously as reclusive as her subaquatic hold, Svetlana's scientific conquests power the world's technological infancy.

An odd friendship with Lorelei Craven directly led to the similarly minded vampires sharing the forefront of the recent chrysmic revolution.

Her castle is **Sunken Citadel** hidden beneath the sea.

***

Eyes-Like-Fire of the **Timberland Plains** is a warrior maiden first and a vampire lord second. The tribal lord, her face riddled with bone piercings and tattoos, is quite happy to abandon her own castle to lead majestic hunts.

Her region, in no small part due to a love for the hunt, experiences a disproportionate count of slain vampire lords. Second in youth and tenure only to Elliott Craven, Eyes-Like-Fire feels a reluctant, distant kinship to him.

Her castle is the **Twilight Gate** atop an unnamed mesa.

***

Mattias Blackburn of **Bleakwood** is the most physically imposing of the vampire lords. As unspoken ruler of the Council of the Eight Holds, his impartiality has kept his more volatile colleagues in line for centuries.

After Lorelei's abdication, his reign is now the longest in the world. Unbeknownst to the rest due to ancient law, he is secretly the father of her children.

His castle is **Blackburn Manor** near a solidified ice lake.

Ooktuk Krum of **Selvara Karn** is the most enigmatic of the vampire lords. Ooktum chooses to listen rather than to speak—with his motives unknown, an air of mystery has enveloped the shamanic lord.

Surrounded by the mystical arts, even temporary allies are nervous of this quiet lord who keeps under control—*somehow*—the most naturally hostile hold in the world.

His castle is **World's Pillar** beneath a gigantic tree.

Chanda Song of **Alevorra** is a fairly new addition to the vampire lords, with a reign under three centuries. Equal in melodic beauty and caustic wit, the sarcastic

Chanda is quick to mock—but slow to support another lord.

The peace across her hold gives Chanda a complete lack of ambition that rivals even Eyes-Like-Fire—but their conflicting hobbies keeps the two from being friends.

Her castle is **Sunstone Temple** in an ancient city ruin.

Valentine Vasiliev of **The Wastes** is an openly brutal and aggressive vampire lord, bordering on malevolence. The second-eldest lord to Akachi Azuzi, these two would make a formidable alliance—if they could ever agree.

Cold and antagonistic as her own bitter hold, Valentine rules an emptier realm than most. With the inexplicable arrival of the human, perhaps she senses *opportunity...*

Her castle is the **Nether Pit** beneath the volcanic tundra.

Made in the USA
Middletown, DE
20 June 2019